"But how are you going to explain?"

Alex sounded confused. "I mean—our being back together again."

"Explain?" Greg seemed surprised she should have thought of such a thing. "We don't explain—why should we? Our private life is very much our own business. If you look at it that way and behave accordingly, there won't be any awkward questions."

A small smile curved Alex's mouth. "Then I'm afraid I shall have to leave it to you to carry off in your usual high-handed manner. I'll just smile as though I think you're the only man in the world."

"Have there been any other men?" he demanded peremptorily.

Alex hung on to her cool remoteness with difficulty. She would have liked to yell "dozens," but she wasn't much good at lies.

Forsaking All Other

Jeneth Murrey

Harlequin Books

TORONTO • NEW YORK • LONDON
AMSTERDAM • PARIS • SYDNEY • HAMBURG
STOCKHOLM • ATHENS • TOKYO • MILAN

Original hardcover edition published in 1983
by Mills & Boon Limited

ISBN 0-373-02567-X

Harlequin Romance first edition August 1983

Printed in the U.S.A.

CHAPTER ONE

'ALEXANDRA!' The tall, dark man halted by the table and calmly slid into the chair opposite her. 'This is an unexpected pleasure, may I get you a drink?' He raised his hand to a passing waiter. 'A whisky for me and a champagne cocktail for the lady,' and then he turned back to her, his dark grey eyes sliding over her without a trace of feeling in their depths. 'And how is my dear wife?' He made the question almost an insult.

Alex fingered the old-fashioned locket which hung on a long gold chain about her neck and then she looked at the crowded club while she thought what to say. Her fingers were not quite steady, but when she spoke, her voice was free from any trace of inward agitation. It was cool, steady and filled with a remote disinterest.

'I'm very well, thank you, Greg,' and she looked past him to where her young sister, Lucy was waltzing with her current escort. The tiny dance floor was packed and Lucy and Robert were taking advantage of the lack of space. They were practically glued together while they moved a step in each direction, which was all that was possible, and Lucy's head was pressed into Robert's shoulder and her eyes were closed. Alex watched them dreamily for a few seconds while she strove for that extra little bit of courage which she always managed to drag up out of nowhere when the going became really rough. She felt it well up inside her so that her pulses ceased their frantic drumming and she knew her face would be serene when she turned back to her husband.

'Your wife? You mean I'm still your wife?' She allowed her eyebrows to rise fractionally. 'I thought you'd have divorced me ages ago,' and then, because she was a woman with a woman's share of curiosity, 'Why didn't you?'

Gregory Mallus, M.A., Ph.D., authority on—and author of numerous books on—the Roman Empire and the influence of Rome on the British Isles, gave her a jeering look before he reached into a pocket for a silver cigarette case, took a cigarette from it, offered it to her as an afterthought and when she shook her head, laid the case down on the table in a prominent position and his lighter flared. The cigarette glowed and the lighter was set down precisely beside the case, then he sat back easily in the chair, tucked his long legs under the table where people passing by wouldn't trip over them and looked at her almost clinically.

It was the kind of inspection he would have given to a piece of pottery or an inscribed stone which had just been dug up; assessing and thoughtful. It took in everything about her from the crown of her pale smooth hair, her oval face, the wide grey-green eyes under her dark winged brows; her small, straight nose and her unexpectedly full, wide mouth.

Alex sat very still with the feeling that she was under some sort of microscope. She wanted desperately to get up and hurry away, but she controlled the impulse, waiting while Greg's glance went on down over her almost too slender figure to the toes of her evening sandals peeping from under the hem of her long black silk evening skirt. There was appreciation in his look and a wicked mockery.

'Now why should I do that?' His eyebrows rose. 'Divorce my wife when you've been so very useful, my dear, even in your absence. Besides, you *must* know that I haven't divorced you—you'd have had the papers served. One cannot divorce a wife in absentia or without letting her know about it. No, my dearest, we're still married. In fact, I keep little mementoes of you about the place.' His hand went out to touch the cigarette case and lighter, a long finger tracing out the monograms cut deeply into the silver.

Alex allowed herself to return the examination and could only come up with three words to describe him, words so trite and overworked that she was reluctant to even think them. 'Mean, moody and magnificent!' Her nose twitched with a small distaste, but she didn't allow his mockery to throw her; she matched it with tartness.

'You keep them for the benefit of your girl-friends when they become importunate, I suppose?'

'Precisely!' He smiled, and it wasn't a nice smile. 'And in addition to all the other bits and pieces, I keep photographs of you, in all the glory of your wedding finery, in the lounge and bedroom. You looked quite beautiful that day . . .'

'. . . And I suppose you draw the said girl-friends' attention to them?'

'I make a point of it,' his smile became lazily

sardonic. 'It emphasises the impermanence of any other relationship.'

'So you're still running true to form. I can't say I'm surprised.' Her soft, wide mouth hardened to an unexpected firmness and her eyes became lit with a cynical gleam. 'I'm so glad I've been of some use.'

The music died away and the hum of conversation rose as the dancers made their way back to the tables. Alex's eyes followed Lucy and Robert as they stopped here and there to exchange words with friends and acquaintances. Greg followed her gaze.

'Little Lucy!' he marvelled. 'And hasn't she developed! I've often wondered what all that girlish loveliness would become. How long is it, my dear—three years or four? And the fellow with her, his face is familiar, don't I know him?' His gaze left Lucy and Robert to return to his wife's face. 'Is he something special?'

'Robert Latchford, and they're talking about marriage,' Alex was curt. 'And it's just three years.' She managed a composed smile and extracted a mirror from her flat evening bag to take a swift look at her reflection. She tut-tutted at the suspicion of a shine on her nose. 'Excuse me for a moment,' she murmured, 'running repairs,' and with a cool dignity, she left the table and headed in the direction of the ladies' powder room.

Once there, she scrabbled around in her bag for the ticket and reclaimed her very ordinary tweed coat. When she heard the music start again, she peeped out of the door. In the dimness, she cast a swift glance at the table where she had been sitting and breathed a sigh of relief that it was empty and unnoticed, then slipped out of the door and made her way out of the club. She halted on the steps outside, feeling like a prisoner who has escaped before the torture began, and stood taking in deep gulps of the cool night air. There was a light drizzle falling and cars and taxis made a wet, hissing sound as they passed, and Alex raised her heated face so that the cool dampness might fall on it.

There wasn't enough money in her purse for a taxi and it was too late for the underground, so she started walking, holding up the hem of her long skirt in an attempt to keep it dry. Just for a few seconds, she cursed her own stupid obstinacy; she could have borrowed some money from either Lucy or Robert if she had been willing to wait, but she hadn't been able to get out of the club quickly enough. In any case, such a request, followed by an abrupt departure, would have involved her in explanations and excuses. She could do without those any time; so now it would be a long walk back to Kensington.

Her evening sandals weren't all that comfortable for walking; the heels were too high and the soles were so thin, they felt as though they were made of paper. In a little while, she judged the straps would be sodden and would start to chafe, but a long, a very long walk was just what she needed, and if her footwear hurt that much, she could always take the sandals off and go barefoot like a penitent. This thought made her mouth curve in a wry smile because, if she did penance, it wouldn't be for her own misdeeds but for Greg's!

Besides, the long walk would give her time to find again that inner calm which she had fought for so long to achieve and which Greg had destroyed this evening with one flick of a black eyebrow.

Alex shook her head sadly and concentrated her thoughts on innocuous things—what to have for dinner the next day, what to wear for work in the morning—so that she didn't notice the rain, the wet pavements or the distance. Oddly enough, it wasn't her meeting with her husband which disturbed her, she could have taken that in her stride—it was the memories which that meeting evoked. She'd buried those memories once before and they hardly ever bothered her now, and what she had done once, she could do again.

A long time ago—was it only three years? It seemed more like a whole lifetime—she had learned her own private lesson. Greg had been her tutor and he had done a thorough job. She would never forget, not completely, but she had learned over the years to push it all into an unused compartment of her mind and shut the door on it firmly.

Alex walked on steadily as she tried to clear her mind. There were so many other things to think about—why dwell on the past with all its bitterness and heartaches? There was Robert's birthday party in a few weeks' time—thank heaven Robert's mother had a big house, because Lucy had come up with a guest list as long as a football pitch. It would have been impossible to cram everybody into the basement flat which was all the two sisters occupied of their house nowadays.

At this point, she became aware of a long black limousine which was creeping along the kerb, keeping pace with her, and she speeded up. The limousine accelerated, swept past her and came to a halt a little in front of her. Greg unfolded himself from behind the wheel, got out on to the pavement and held the door open for her.

'Get in!' It was a harsh command.

'Thank you, but no.' Alex took two or three paces which brought her level with him while she schooled her face to a cool mask that betrayed nothing of her inward feelings. 'It's a pleasant night,' she temporised, dragging the tweed coat more closely about her and dismissing the drizzle and the wet pavements with a small, mirthless smile. 'I'd rather walk, I can do with the fresh air.'

'Fresh air!' He looked at her as though she had gone mad and his hand went to her shoulder and tightened on it, ignoring her involuntary flinch. 'Your coat's wet through, so's your hair, and how much further do you think you can walk in those stupid shoes? Get *in*!' Through the damp tweed, she could feel the power of his fingers. '*In!*' he reiterated as he forced her towards the open door of the car.

It would be undignified to struggle—her mind flicked around and ahead. The street was empty, but—she recalled part of a conversation from earlier in the evening when Robert had been explaining some 'Law' to her and Lucy. She didn't remember very much about it, not even its name, because she hadn't been listening properly; Robert sometimes prosed on in a very uninteresting fashion. Lucy, of course, listened to every word that fell from his lips, but Lucy was in love with him, which made a difference; she would have listened while he read out the whole contents of a telephone directory. Alex was not in love with him, so she just heard him, letting only the bare bones of the 'Law' penetrate.

According to this 'Law', things always happened when it was most inconvenient. If one was late, the bus or train went early, and conversely, if one was early, the bus was late. If one gambled when one couldn't afford it, one lost; if one wished for peace and quiet, one found oneself in the middle of a noisy crowd. If you were prepared for any emergency, no emergency arose, but on the other hand, if you weren't prepared, that was the time that the emergency fell on you like a ton of bricks!

Alex glanced up and down the empty street. It was empty now, but if Robert's 'Law' was to be believed, she only had to make a fuss and it would immediately be filled with interested passers-by and a policeman or two. She entered the car unwillingly. It was an American model with a left-hand drive, and she found herself staring at the steering wheel and a complicated instrument panel.

'Do you expect me to drive this?' she demanded in a voice which would have frozen the fur off a Polar bear.

'No—move over.' His harsh voice grated on her ears and she slid along the bench type seat, bunching her skirt to keep it away from the automatic gear stick. Greg slid in after her and put out a hand to the ignition switch.

'Kensington, isn't it?'

'Yes.' She concentrated her attention on the car; it was very large, much too large for driving around London, but Greg always had liked big foreign cars. But even this vastness was too small for herself and him. It was too dark, too warm, too intimate. Alex leaned back in her seat, trying to build an impervious wall about herself out of nothing but her own will power.

'The same house.' The interior light had extinguished itself and his voice came to her in the little darkness which was illuminated only by the glow of the instrument panel. He wasn't asking a question, and she wondered if he'd been having her watched or had been keeping tabs on her in some other way. Three years was a long time, she could quite easily have moved.

'Yes.' Her own coolness surprised her, she had thought she might sound wobbly and insecure, but since she sounded quite composed, she let words spill over in banal chatter. 'It's different now—the house, I mean. We had a proper conversion done just over two years ago and it's now four self-contained flats. The top two are let out, Aunt Ermine has the ground floor and Lucy and I have the basement.'

'The basement?' Greg made it sound like a prison cell and, stealing a quick look at his face in the light of a street lamp, Alex thought she detected a look of distaste. She hastened to correct any wrong impression he might have gained from his visits to the house in the past.

'Mmm.' She was beginning to feel better and talking about quite ordinary things came easily to her. 'I think I've made it look quite nice. What

used to be the old kitchen and servants' parlour
has been knocked into one and it's now our
kitchen-cum-diner and lounge. It faces south, so
it's sunny all day, and it looks out on to the
garden at the back.'

Abruptly, he changed the subject. 'It's a damn
long way to Kensington.' He drew the car into the
kerb, switched on the interior light and, before she
realised his intentions, he had reached across,
opened the bag that lay in her lap and emptied the
contents on to the black silk of her skirt. He
flicked aside comb, compact, tissues, keys and
handkerchiefs to pick up the small purse with its
few coins. Carefully he counted them into his
palm.

'And you *were* going to walk!' He made it sound
unbelievable. 'Aren't you carrying independence a
bit too far, or are you so bloody-minded you can't
help it?'

Alex closed her eyes wearily. It had always been
this way with Greg; he exhausted her, drained her
of even the power to think properly. She'd thought
she was over it. Over it! If three years hadn't made
any difference, neither would thirteen or thirty.
She would be like this until she died, and he called
it bloody-minded!

The car resumed its journey and eventually slid
to a halt, but Alex didn't notice. Her eyes were
closed and she was in a waking, dreaming state, a
limbo between heaven and hell where pleasure
only led to unimaginable pain and there was no
hope left.

'Out! Keys!' Greg was being monosyllabic, and
when she didn't move, he once more groped in her

bag and his fingers on her arm tightened as she made a move to stop him. The grip was painful, but it was even more painful when, after giving an exasperated grunt, he came round the car and opened the door on her side to reach in and grasp her. 'Out!' he commanded again, and she was standing on the wet pavement and he was almost dragging her across it to the flight of stone steps that led up to the door, She halted with one foot on the bottom step, stiffening herself against his impelling hand.

'No, not that door. Ermine might be disturbed, she hears every little sound.' She gestured instead to the area steps which led down from a gate in the railings. 'I told you, Lucy and I have the basement.'

'And why do you have to occupy the basement? It's your house, isn't it? Why couldn't you have had the ground floor instead of living like a troglodyte?'

'Don't you ever listen when I tell you something?' Temper flared in her and she became cross. 'Because of the entrance hall, the ground floor flat is the smallest in the house, just three rooms and a bathroom. It's too small for Lucy and me,' and then, because he was hurting her arm and there would be bruises tomorrow, 'You can let me go now. I'm here, which is where I could run to, there's no place else.' And she turned down the flight of steps.

Greg followed her down, brushing past her at the door to slide the key in the lock and push the heavy door open. Alex slipped past him and led the way down the passage to the kitchen, hurrying so that there would be less chance of him touching her. She walked straight through without bothering to switch on a light, but Greg, following her, slid his hand down the wall to find the switch. There was a click and the room flooded with light.

As she had said, it was a pleasant room; the kitchen units arranged under the wide window which in daytime would give a view out over the small garden, and the diner-cum-lounge was on a slightly higher level. The switch which Greg had operated controlled the fluorescent strip lighting in the kitchen area, the bright light threw everything into sharp relief, and it wasn't kind to Alex. It highlighted the angles of her too thin face and body, shone through her make-up to show shadows under her long grey-green eyes and turned her blonde hair to silver.

'Get out of that wet coat.' Again he was giving orders, and she watched him as he filled the kettle, plugged it in and switched on. She opened her mouth to protest, decided against it and closed it again as he threw words at her over his shoulder. 'You're looking your age and a bit more, Alex. What's the matter, have you been ill?'

''Flu,' she answered him automatically as she shed her coat, letting it fall and lie across the back of a chair. 'Three weeks ago,' she amplified, 'but I'm over it now.'

Greg was making tea in a rather incompetent way, and she winced as cups and saucers rattled on the counter top and things started falling out of the cupboards when he opened them, but he kept his back to her, which was a good thing, as it gave her more time to pull herself together. When he brought the tray to a small table beside her chair she was superficially composed, her pale face a mask with no expression painted upon it.

'Why?' she asked.

'Why what?' He was giving her no help, his dark face was impassive and his grey eyes were half hidden under his heavy lids. Alex noticed that there were some grey threads at his temples, they were brushed back severely with the rest of his hair so that they formed silvery streaks in the blackness. He hadn't had those three years ago and his hair was shorter now as well; it no longer curled just above his collar. Apart from that, he hadn't changed much, his face was seemingly ageless and it revealed very little of what was going on inside him, and although he was tall and powerfully built, he was still athletically slim with no sign of a bulge anywhere. But then there wouldn't be; he was only—Alex did a rapid mental calculation—thirty-six, nearly thirty-seven, just a little over ten years older than herself, and in any case, he wasn't the type that ran to fat. When Greg aged, he would get thinner. Just at present, though, he was very good to look at, and her eyes slid fondly over the well-cut dinner jacket which took away some of the massiveness from his shoulders.

Alex found her gaze lingering on him and was glad that all his attention was given to pouring out tea so that he didn't notice she was staring at him like a starving thing looking at a plate of food. She hastily averted her gaze and took great interest in a spot, just over the top of his head where a perfectly ordinary calendar was hanging.

'Why have you come now? What do you want of me?' She wrinkled her brow and reached for the sugar bowl, spooning sugar into her tea lavishly and making it far too sweet. 'After three years of silence, you suddenly pop up like the Demon King in pantomime. You must want something, but I'm warning you, you're wasting your time. I owe you nothing and I want nothing from you.'

'Not even an explanation—bah!' He made a sharp chopping motion with his hand. 'You'd never get one from me, I never explain.'

'You don't have to.' Alex took a sip from her cup and then sat looking down into it as though it was a crystal ball that contained the past. 'The whole thing, everything that happened, was self-explanatory. Anything you could have said would only have made it worse. Forget it, that's my advice,' she smiled wanly. 'You wouldn't show to advantage making excuses for yourself.'

'You walked out on me.' Greg's mouth twisted in a wry smile.

'And did that prick your conceit a little? Oh dear, I'm so sorry, but did you honestly believe I was so besotted that I wouldn't see straight ever again?' She kept her eyes down and stirred the tea, concentrating on the surface of the liquid.

'Look at me,' he demanded.

'No.' She tapped the side of the cup with the spoon, refusing to raise her head.

'You're frightened!'

'And why not?' She was almost speaking to herself. 'You've a whale of a reputation and I give you full marks for charming birds from trees. I shouldn't stand a chance against you, and you know it—that was one reason why I got out from under. No, Greg,' she smiled at him sadly and lowered her eyes to the table again, 'I promised myself that I'd never let you con me again. Go back to your willing ladies, there are dozens of them, and maybe they believe what you tell them. I don't, not any longer. I can't think why you bothered with me in the first place, I was way out of your class.'

She shivered as she recalled her first encounters with Greg. They hadn't been exactly auspicious, but there had been nothing about them to hint that they presaged the brief heaven or the present hell she was suffering.

The secretarial agency for which she had worked had sent her to him as a typist, and the manageress had been apologetic as she had handed over the card with his name and address.

'Not one of our best natured customers,' she had grimaced. 'Would you believe, he went through every girl on the books before we fixed him up with Molly. He reduced most of them to tears in a few days. I was thinking of giving out medals to anybody who'd put up with him for more than a week. He's expecting Molly again.'

'It'd be a bit difficult now,' Alex had chuckled as she accepted the card, and she was still smiling to herself when she had knocked at the door of Greg's Chelsea flat.

'Who are you?' He had let her in but made no move to make her feel welcome. His eyebrows were a black bar across the top of his commanding nose and he had looked at her down the length of it. 'Your manageress knows better than to fob me off with a junior. I want Molly.'

Alex had faced him squarely. 'So does a man called Jim,' she had told him, 'and he's getting her as soon as the plane lands in Sydney.'

Greg had run long, sensitive fingers through his black hair. It hadn't been very tidy to start with and by the time he had handcombed it, it resembled a large, untidy bird's nest. 'I'll wait for her to return,' he had said decidedly. 'The work is very important and exacting.'

Alex had composed her face into a judicious expression. 'You'll wait a long time,' and she had lowered her head to hide the mirth in her eyes. 'You may have a manuscript, but Jim has a—a station, I think it's called, hundreds of square miles and millions of sheep. He'll also have a marriage licence in his pocket when he meets that plane. Now, if you'll show me where I'm to work, I'd like to get started. You're paying for my time and I don't like wasting it.'

Alex had worked for him for nearly ten months before she allowed herself to admit that she loved him, and even then she hadn't been ecstatic about it. He wasn't the sort of man she wanted to love, she had always envisaged a cosy, comfortable marriage, but that wasn't the sort of relationship Greg had in mind. He had explained himself and his desires briefly and, in case there should be any doubt, in words of not more than two syllables.

Alex had countered his proposition equally briefly. 'I don't want an affair, thank you; it isn't my scene. I'm old-fashioned and very narrow-minded, also I have a young sister, and I wouldn't like to set her a bad example.' And she had gone back to her typing, outwardly calm but inwardly full of misgivings. She was still full of them three months later when they were married. Greg might be an egghead, but he was a very attractive egghead, and to her certain knowledge he had never practised self-denial or abstinence. She brooded about how he would cope with anything as confining as marriage, and also how she would cope with him when he occasionally let himself off the chain.

But at least, she had comforted herself, she was marrying the man she loved. She mightn't approve of him, but she loved him—so that when she said 'I will' it was in a firm tone although she had kept her fingers crossed. The marriage had lasted three weeks precisely, three weeks of hard slogging work while Alex had typed out the last chapters of Greg's book, and then they were to have gone on a short honeymoon, but on the morning they were due to fly out to the States, Ermine had rung—would Alex come over straight away, Lucy was ill.

Greg had piled all the luggage in the car and they had stopped off at the Kensington house, where Lucy had been in bed in a darkened room and Ermine had been on the verge of hysterics. Greg had taken one look at the patient and diagnosed a hangover, which Lucy had denied vigorously, or as vigorously as she could, and Alex had believed her.

'I can't leave her, not like this.' Alex had been appalled at his hardheartedness. 'Can't we put off the trip for a couple of days?'

'A matter of priorities.' Greg had been terse with her. 'I'm catching that plane. Whether you come with me or not is entirely up to you,' and Alex had tried to be reasonable.

'She's only sixteen, Greg, and she needs me. Ermine works from nine till five, you know that, there'll be nobody to look after her. I must stay.' And Greg had walked out, out of the house and out of her life. She hadn't believed it at first, comforting herself with the thought that as soon as he was over his temper he would see her side of it and ring. She had waited for him, spending the next few days never more than a few feet from the phone and slowly freezing up inside. He didn't ring, and her bright future vanished, leaving her cold and lonely.

Alex's world had been in fragments about her feet and the rebuilding of it was a long and painful process, but at least she managed it. She went back to work for the secretarial agency and immersed herself in work. Work was supposed to be a cure for everything. Alex found that it wasn't a cure, but it did help. It didn't give her much time to read the papers or to examine the photographs of Greg, usually accompanied by some lovely, and she tried not to listen when Lucy read out the jucier pieces to her. But now she knew the value of those painful years.

They had been worth nothing at all! One look from Greg and her hardwon peace was shattered, the pain was back, only this time it hurt worse than ever.

With a start, she came back to the present, accepting the situation, accepting the fact that she still loved him, that she always would, but knowing as well that his sort of love wasn't good enough for her. It was too selfish, too narrow. She wanted, she needed more than he could give her. Theirs, she told herself, had been a love that stood no chance of long-term success. It had grown, flowered and fruited too quickly, it lacked a nice stable background. She had gone into it with too little thought, swept off her feet by the magic of it so that good sense and reason went flying out of the window.

It wasn't all Greg's fault. A lot of the blame must be hers!

CHAPTER TWO

ALEX came back to the present with a shiver and raised her eyes from her tea-cup. The tea had cooled so that it was no longer drinkable and she pushed it aside.

'Thank you for bringing me home.' She said it sedately like a small child thanking a grown-up for a not very exciting present. 'Goodnight!'

'Not so fast, Alexandra,' and she winced. Why did he sometimes use her full name instead of the shortened form? He was the only person who had ever done that, and in the old days he had made it sound like a caress. To hear it again after so long hurt her abominably. She looked up at him, noticing that he made no attempt to take the hint that he wasn't welcome. He sat there opposite her on the tall stool he had hitched across from its place by the kitchen counter, and he looked immovable. His eyes sought hers and there was a warning glitter in their depths. 'I haven't finished yet, my dear.'

So it was to be a battle—mentally she armed herself with a remote bitterness. 'A pity,' her sneer was delicately feminine, 'because I finished with you three years ago.'

'So you like to think,' there was a soft menace in his words which made them more frightening than an open threat, 'but if you think that, you're mistaken. No,' he held up his hand and waved her

24

to silence, 'I'm only basing my opinions on your own actions, Alex. If you found me that offensive, you could have sued for divorce but you didn't, and as for the life I led after we split up, you could hardly pretend to surprise, could you? I never made any attempt to hide my past misdeeds from you.'

There were a lot of words bubbling on the back of her tongue, but she suppressed them, contenting herself with what she hoped was an icy glare and chilly phrasing.

'Your past! I gagged at swallowing that, Greg, but as you pointed out, it *was* the past, so I choked it down. That's all over and I promised once that I'd never remind you of it. No, it's what has gone on since. An ex-mistress or so I could stomach, but not ongoing affairs. You walked out at the first hint that I wasn't going to obey your slightest whim and you've been behaving like a rutting stag ever since. Give me the evidence, names, times and places and I'll get busy, but you could more easily divorce me, couldn't you? It would be a straight case of incompatibility, that's the usual thing nowadays and we *are* incompatible, we proved that three years ago.'

'Make it easy for you, you mean,' he raised an eyebrow. 'Then you could go back to being the virginal Miss Winter without any loss of face and all the nasty details swept under the carpet. Oh no, my girl! You say we're incompatible, that's the funniest thing I ever heard. You didn't even try! Three weeks, that's all we had, and if you call that a sensible probation period, I don't. No, I'm not handing it to you on a plate like that, I have other ideas.'

Alex's temper started to rise and she felt more confident. Fighting helped to numb the pain and saying hard, hurtful things helped as well. Thinking them up and spitting them out occupied her mind so completely that there was no room left for yesterday's regrets and sorrows. She even stopped feeling the tiny prick of guilt that stabbed at her when she remembered that she had put Lucy and Ermine first. She thought hard, mentally rehearsed the words and let them drip from her tongue in a bitter stream.

'When did you ever hand me anything on a plate? You took advantage of me, of my inexperience, and when you couldn't get me any other way, you sacrificed your precious freedom—but not for too long, oh no! And,' she allowed herself a momentary digression, 'I don't think very much of your latest *chère amie*, the one you had two months ago. She looked definitely second or third hand, and I thought you preferred virgins.'

Alex had hoped that this would make him lose his temper and perhaps storm out, but she was disappointed. He sat on the stool, looking at her appreciatively through a drift of cigarette smoke and smiling wickedly as he contemplated the glowing tip of his cigarette.

'Better and better, Alex, I give you full marks— you certainly have come out of your shell. You've just said "virgin" without even the trace of a blush—there's hope for you yet! You couldn't have done that three years ago.'

'I've been practising,' she told him hardily, 'taking a few lessons from the younger generation.

Lucy's been coaching me.'

'In that case, what I have to say to you shouldn't offend your sensibilities too much.' Greg was laughing at her, and it made her mad. 'You walked out—no, don't try and butt in till I've finished. I didn't say you walked out on me; I said, or I was going to say, that you walked out on our marriage—now I think it's time you walked back again.'

'Not while I have breath,' she assured him, her temper flaring so that her eyes glittered with sparks of green among the icy grey chips and her soft mouth hardened. 'You can divorce me, I'm only sorry it can't be a straightforward annulment. In fact, you can do whatever you like so long as I'm rid of you, but . . .'

'. . . But I'm sure you'll change your mind, all the signs are favourable for a resumption of our marital relationship.' Greg stood up, taking a swift glance around the room, and his eyes finally fell on what he was looking for. Two strides took him to the counter under the window and he reached for the idiot board hanging there. Underneath the jottings—rice, tomatoes, brown sugar, coffee—he scrawled a number. 'That's the telephone number of the new flat, I decided we'd need something a little bigger—you can ring me there when you change your mind.' He came back to her and bent over to tilt her chin in his fingers.

Alex flinched away from him, but he merely laughed and she felt the humiliation of having him discover just how much his touch upset her. Greg had always been fond of physical contact and, once upon a time, she too had thought it heavenly, but not any more. Now it made her shiver.

He laughed again, but it wasn't a real laugh, there was no amusement in it, only a hint of triumph and as he brought his face close to hers. Alex kept her eyes open, seeing the white patches that betokened temper by his nostrils, and then, when his face came too close, she closed her eyes automatically and his mouth was on hers. A hard, angry mouth, that bruised her lips savagely, forcing them apart and making her eyes water with the pain of it.

Her hands raised to push him away, but they were as traitorous as the rest of her body. Instead they wandered up around his shoulders and found their way to the nape of his neck and her fingers threaded through his hair. She was bitterly ashamed of the ease with which he could still stir her and she caught at the bitterness, holding on to it, dwelling on it to increase her self-disgust so that finally she found the strength to push him away and turn her face into the cushioned back of the chair.

'Oh yes.' He was looking down at her—she knew that although her head was turned away from him. She knew also that his eyes would be lit with an exultant gleam and the thought made her want to weep. 'You'll be back, Alex, and this time we'll give it a proper chance, we'll get the priorities right. As I said, ring when you change your mind. I wouldn't like to be otherwise engaged on such an auspicious occasion.'

'I won't.' Even though she felt emotionally exhausted, defiance still flickered. 'Never!'

He was at the kitchen door and he turned and

gave her a mocking grin. 'Don't say "never", my love—you forget, I know you very well and I can put my finger on your Achilles heel whenever I want.' And he walked out of the room and along the passage to the door.

When he was gone and she heard the thud of the outside door as he slammed it behind him, Alex dragged herself out of her chair feeling as though she had been physically assaulted. She ached all over so that it was an effort to go to the counter and switch the kettle back on to make herself another cup of tea. Now that she was alone and she no longer had to put on a show, her misery increased. It returned in full force and she found herself almost wishing that Greg was still here and they were still exchanging insults. At least, while that had been happening, she had felt alive.

For three years she had taught herself to hate him, she had dwelled on his selfishness, his insensitivity and any other bad qualities she could think of until she was sickened and had to stop thinking of him in sheer self-defence. As far as she was concerned, Greg Mallus was a nightmare from her past, but this evening he'd walked out of that past to become reality again and he was behaving as if he intended to be the corner stone of her future. He had called her a masochist once, but surely she wasn't that fond of self-inflicted pain that she could be coerced into a life of it; it didn't bear thinking of.

She switched on the kettle and then switched it off again automatically as her hand went to the side of the fat teapot. She'd already made tea and she didn't really want what she'd made—Greg had upset her so much that she could no longer think straight. With a laugh that bordered on the hysterical, she emptied away the tea, tidied up the counter and went along the passage to her bedroom.

There had been no satisfaction in her verbal battle with her husband and she decided that Robert's 'Law' was quite correct. While Greg had been with her and she had needed to find the correct words to enable her to tell him exactly what she thought of him, of his behaviour, of his arrogant assumption that he was right; the words had escaped her and she had put up a very poor show. Now that he was gone, all the telling phrases, all the hurtful epithets came crowding into her mind and they came too late to be of any use!

It was all too late anyway, three years too late, and with a sigh, Alex showered and slid into bed. It was at times like this that she could have done with a bit of sympathetic company or perhaps somebody bracing and optimistic who would force her to look on the bright side. Neither Lucy nor Ermine came into the category she required; Lucy was too full of her own romance to spare a thought for anyone else and Ermine—here Alex made a rueful grimace—Ermine was an echo who would agree with everything Alex said.

She could imagine the conversation. She would say, 'Greg is a beast, little better than a wild animal and with the same instincts,' and Ermine would reply, 'Yes, dear,' in sickly-sweet agreement.

Dully, she supposed that tonight would be another disturbed and unsatisfactory night when she would wake from a dream of being with Greg to find herself alone. If that was so, the sooner she went to sleep the better; she would get it over quickly. So she punched viciously at her pillows, battering them into comfort, and then closed her eyes, mutely resigned to whatever was to come.

Alex woke to Lucy's hammering on the bedroom door and her loud shout of, 'Come *on*, Alex. It's seven o'clock!' Alex groaned and resisted the temptation to turn over, bury her head beneath the duvet and go back to sleep again. This morning was one of those mornings when everything seemed too much. To her surprise, she had dropped off to sleep without any difficulty, but Lucy had delayed her return home until nearly three in the morning, and Lucy was incapable of being quiet about anything. Doors slammed, things fell or were knocked over, the shower hissed like a cageful of angry snakes and Lucy sang loudly all through her ablutions. Yet here she was at seven in the morning, full of life and bouncing with enthusiasm after less than four hours' sleep. She was worse than Pippa!

With a despairing grunt, Alex heaved herself out of bed and hurried off to the bathroom. Her reflection in the mirror wasn't comforting, although it hadn't been a bad night; her face showed the strain of coping with Greg and the pale violet shadows beneath her eyes would require more than the usual smear of foundation to cover them. Even her hair looked lank and lifeless. She hurried through a shower to allow more time for her face and when she at last entered the kitchen, dressed, made up and ready for work, the strain hardly showed.

Lucy was piling bread into the toaster and Alex raised her eyebrows at this unaccustomed activity.

'You're early.'

'Mmm,' Lucy went on with making coffee. 'I wanted to have a bit of a talk before we had to rush off.' She raised her head and smiled winningly, and Alex wilted and shrank into insignificance. It was always the same when she stood by Lucy! Lucy's golden hair, rich and thick, made her own pale tresses look anaemic; her sister's wide blue eyes made her own grey-green ones almost colourless and Lucy's well rounded figure turned her own slender elegance into an unattractive scragginess. 'Sit down,' Lucy whisked herself away to the toaster. 'I'll do it—oh damn!' she uttered in a muffled tone as the door opened and Ermine entered.

'Good morning, Aunty.' Lucy's eyes sparkled with aggravation. 'So nice of you to join us—you should have come earlier, I'd have made an extra lot of toast.' She said it with relish, knowing very well that Ermine hated the 'Aunty', and Alex sighed with frustration. Lucy and Ermine had never got on well together, it was one reason why Lucy always stressed the relationship. For Alex, it was different. Ermine had been her father's youngest sister, barely ten years old when Alex was born, and to a casual observer, Alex and Ermine looked more like sisters than did Alex and Lucy. They had the same pale hair, the same light eyes, although the green was predominant in Ermine's and they shared the same slimness. The only thing Ermine and Lucy had in common was a lack of inches; they were both several inches shorter than herself. 'I was hoping for a private talk with Alex.' Lucy was almost rude.

'Good morning, Lucy,' Ermine smiled gently, and forgave her younger niece's bad manners. 'You were coming in very late last night, or rather this morning.'

'Just before three.' Lucy was unconcerned as she spread butter lavishly on her toast and then scraped most of it off again, muttering 'Calories'. 'Were you watching at the window as usual, Aunty? I hope so, because I gave Robert a particularly passionate kiss just for your benefit.'

Ermine ignored the baiting, she knew she was no match for her younger niece when it came to a battle of words. Lucy could be incredibly rude and crude when she was in the mood and she wasn't handicapped by any consideration or respect for age or experience.

'I saw you come in as well, Alex.' Ermine's mouth curved into a smile of delight. 'I'm so pleased you feel better, well enough for an evening out, although I think you should still be careful ... the night air ... It would be better if you took some time off work and went out in the daylight. Who was the man? He had rather a splendid car, although, to my mind, it was so big as to be vulgar.'

'It was Greg,' Alex said dismissively, and buried her nose in her coffee cup.

'Greg? But I thought. . . .'

'Come off it, Aunty!' Lucy spoke inelegantly through a mouthful of toast. 'Greg's Alex's husband, she can come home with him if she wants to.' She consulted her calorie chart and decided against marmalade. 'I know they fell out, but that was years ago, there's no reason why they can't be friends now, if they want to.'

'They fell out, as you put it, because of you.' Ermine was waspish.

'That's right, blame me,' Lucy muttered it defiantly.

'Indeed, I do blame you,' her aunt was virtuous. 'If you hadn't lied about having too much to drink . . .'

'So what?' Lucy was unrepentant. 'I don't lie very often, do I?' she appealed to Alex, 'but I felt so ghastly and I knew that Aunty dear would raise the roof and lock me up every evening. Anyway, Greg told Alex what was the matter with me, and if she'd had any sense, she'd have believed him.'

Alex thought it was time to interfere. 'Stop it, both of you!'

Ermine smiled understandingly, 'Certainly, dear, but you must admit that there are times when Lucy is quite impossible, she has no idea of how to behave . . .'

'. . . And speaking of behaviour,' Lucy interrupted what was turning into a catalogue of her bad points, almost shouting her aunt down, 'kindly remember I don't spy on people! You must have known that it was Greg last night, my dear old aunt; because Alex left the club well before midnight and the street lighting would have still been on when she arrived here. Or didn't you have enough time to focus your binoculars?' She finished off her coffee with a gulp and stood up. 'Well, that's my rations, so I'm off to the Flower

Power shop. Ta-ta, everybody, I'll phone and let you know what I'm doing this evening.' And she picked up her jacket and went out, her candy-striped pink skirt swinging about her legs.

'Well!' Ermine gasped as she at last sat down, and from somewhere, Alex conjured up a smile.

'Don't pay too much attention to her,' she advised. 'She's only saying things to try to shock you.'

'But there's no shame in her,' Ermine protested. 'You'd think she'd be just a little ashamed if only for getting drunk at that age—how old? Not a day over sixteen, it's illegal!'

'We all make mistakes,' Alex soothed, 'and Lucy has one great virtue; she never makes the same mistake twice.'

'But if it hadn't been for her. . . .'

'. . . It would have been something else.' Alex rose and went round the table to put a comforting arm about her aunt's slender shoulders.

'What did he want?' Ermine poured herself a cup of coffee. 'Sit down, Alex, we've plenty of time this morning.'

Alex refused to be drawn. 'Why, nothing, dear. I wanted to leave, it was raining and I hadn't sufficient money for a cab and I didn't want to spoil Lucy's evening, so Greg gave me a lift. There was no more to it than that—and Lucy's quite right, you know. Greg and I can meet and be pleasantly friendly, lots of separated couples do, it's what's known as civilised behaviour.' She was matter-of-fact, but her mouth twisted wryly on the last words.

'Well, all I hope is that you don't let him hurt

you again.' Ermine finished her coffee and rose. 'Now I must be off—such a bore on a lovely spring day, sitting in that office, coping with Income Tax.'

'Nonsense, you love it,' Alex manufactured a smile. 'It gives you a feeling of power, being able to haul big, strong men over the coals and saying "Pay up or else!" '

Alex went off to work quite happily, or as happily as she ever did anything nowadays. She was temping at a small factory in the outer suburbs and the work was far from exacting; by twelve o'clock she had finished everything there was to do and she was just contemplating whether to take an early lunch when her telephone rang.

'I want to see you.' Lucy sounded upset. 'I've an extra hour for lunch today. It was supposed to be my half day, but one of the other girls hasn't come in and I have to work this afternoon and I may not be home this evening. I'll meet you outside your place for lunch.' And she rang off abruptly.

Alex grew thoughtful. Lucy had sounded rather cross, but she was given to little rages when she met opposition. Perhaps Robert's mother was objecting to the enormous number of people whom Lucy thought it necessary to invite to his party. To Lucy, a party was just that—as many people as could be crammed in, and she didn't care if there weren't enough chairs or the food ran out. Whereas Robert's mother was a bit of a stickler for doing things properly.

She calculated that she had a good half hour before Lucy could arrive, and she made use of it, brushing her hair and dragging it back into a ponytail redoing her face with a warmer coloured foundation and using a slightly darker lipstick and flicking with a brush to remove some specks from her sober clerical grey suit. When arguing with Lucy, Alex found it better to give the appearance of being totally in command of both herself and the situation, her young sister was inclined to take advantage of anything which would give her the upper hand.

At last, when she was satisfied with her appearance, she left the office and went across the small yard to the gates where Lucy was waiting for her, a foot tapping with ill concealed irritation.

'I've been waiting ages!' Lucy's blue eyes weren't smiling, her soft, bee-stung mouth was nearly a straight line and her whole air was one of grim determination. 'Blast Aunty! I wanted to talk to you at breakfast, but I didn't get a chance. Come on, is this where you eat?' and she headed for the small restaurant opposite at a swift pace.

'It isn't so very much I asked.' Lucy hardly gave them time to be seated before she started talking. 'I thought you'd understand, that you'd see things my way—after all, you're always saying you'd do whatever's best for me. I was relying on you, but when I rang Greg this morning, he said that you'd said "No", and after all the trouble I went to, to get him and you together in that club last night!'

'Lucy!' Alex looked round hastily, but the restaurant was empty except for themselves. 'I don't know what you're talking about. Would you mind starting back at the beginning, please. What's this about getting Greg and me together?'

'I fixed it up.' Her sister looked rather pleased

with herself. 'And after I'd explained everything to him and he could see how necessary it was, he said he'd find an opportunity to have a talk with you. He's quite willing, so why are you being awkward? I'm not asking anything very much!'

'The beginning,' Alex insisted. 'What exactly do you want, and *why*?' Her mouth tightened as she looked at her sister's flushed face. 'If you don't give me a straight explanation immediately, I'm walking out, and you can stew.'

'Oh, all right,' Lucy avoided her gaze. 'It's a bit of a long story, though—you know how Robert's mother has always thought I'm not quite good enough for him, always telling me about his other girl-friends like the one that's the daughter of a Q.C. and that girl he knows whose father runs a stable at Newmarket, she's an awful snob, Robert's mother, I mean . . . well, one day she was showing me a photograph in one of her magazines—it was Greg with some woman in Rome and there was the usual blurb. Robert's mother was all excited, apparently the Malluses used to live next door or something like that, and she was all gooey about him, how this woman in the photograph was a countess or something and she said they would probably get married, so I said . . .'

'You said he couldn't . . .' Alex sighed in despair.

'That's right—honestly, Alex, it wasn't my fault, I didn't intend . . . I just said he was married to my sister . . .'

'And how did you explain that I didn't live with him?'

'Easy,' Lucy grinned. 'I said that when he was out of the country, you always lived with me, it saved you being lonely.'

'Thank you!' Alex was bitter. 'And did this revelation make you more acceptable? Did it make your love affair run more smoothly?'

'Much easier.' Lucy breathed a sigh of relief.

'And how were you going to explain things, like when he came back to London and we didn't . . . I still stayed in Kensington . . .?'

'I didn't look that far ahead,' Lucy admitted, 'but when he did come back, I got in touch with him straight away. I told him all about it and he was great—I can't think why you dislike him so much, Alex, I think he's fabulous—we fixed up the meeting in the club. He knows Robert's mother, knows what she's like, he understood! Oh, come on, Alex, it wouldn't hurt you to do what I want, would it? You'd only have to move back to his flat for a while, he said it was all up to you, he'd go along with whatever you decided, and you will, won't you? I know you will!'

Alex looked at her sister's face and was shocked to see how it had grown up in the last few hours. This wasn't the face of a carefree girl, not any more; it was the face of a frightened young woman, somebody who was seeing the bright future turning into loss and unhappiness. She must have looked like that once herself, she knew the feeling, the hurting sadness, the sense of loss . . .

Lucy's soft mouth had firmed. 'You see,' she explained seriously, 'I've worked hard on Robert, he's just what I want, and we'll have a good life, I know we will. It would kill me to lose him now, and I've worked hard on his mother as well, making her like me, because she didn't, not at first. Alex, you can't mess things up for me!'

'No, that wouldn't be either sensible or kind.' Now that it was all out in the open, Alex became calm. Her thin, sensitive fingers went out to touch Lucy's plump, soft, white ones, touching the diamond and sapphire star which was new to her. 'Is this an engagement ring?'

'Mmm.' Lucy looked at it proudly. 'But it's a secret until the party—that's when we're going to tell his mother—so you see . . .'

'Yes, I see.' Alex managed a smile which was almost natural. 'I'm sorry that everything isn't arranged yet,' and she tried very hard to keep a faint sarcasm out of her voice. 'Greg and I didn't have much chance to talk last night, but he did suggest that we give it another try—our marriage, I mean. But you have to understand that was something I had to think about, it's a big step.'

'Oh!' Lucy digested this information, her grief and worry, like a summer shower, nearly over and the sun was coming out for her. 'No,' she decided when Alex offered her the menu, 'I won't have any lunch, I'll go straight back to the shop. What a relief, I feel like dancing all the way! Perhaps I should, the exercise would be good for me.' She was on her feet now and her eyes were sparkling. 'I do envy you, Alex. You can eat like a horse and never get any fatter, while I have to watch every calorie. I'm petrified I'm going to bulge in my wedding dress!' and she was gone, flying out of the restaurant on light feet.

Alex sat alone at the table, ordered, and when

the food arrived she applied herself to ham and salad. She didn't want to eat, each mouthful felt as though it would choke her, but she'd had less than half a slice of toast for breakfast and going without lunch wouldn't help a bit. She would be drained of energy and exhausted before the battle with Greg began. Already she knew what the price would be, he had told her last night; but why?

None of it made any sense, and she gloomily pushed her plate aside in favour of a cup of strong black coffee while she tried to work it out. The only thing she could think of was that his pride was smarting and he was determined that she should pay for it—but on the other hand, that didn't accord with the Greg she had known so well. He'd been bad-tempered and irascible, but never small-minded, never concerned with the look of things, but ... Here she paused. Perhaps he'd been immersed in the Roman scene for so long, he'd started thinking like Nero or Caligula!

Diplomatically, she begged the afternoon off and went straight back to the house in Kensington. In the kitchen of the basement flat everything was calm and serene and she would have no interruptions. Ermine wouldn't be home until after five o'clock, and at this juncture, Alex could very well do without her aunt's searching questions. Ermine would want to know why, and that would land Lucy in another lot of trouble.

The telephone number was still on the idiot board and her fingers were perfectly steady as she dialled it. While she listened to the ringing tone, she held up her hand to the light and marvelled at her calm until she realised that ever since the previous evening she had been filled with a fear that something unpleasant was going to happen, almost as though she was a prisoner on trial and awaiting the verdict; whether she would be condemned or, by some wild chance, get off scot free. Now she knew! The 'something unpleasant' *had* happened and the verdict had gone against her, so all that was left was a matter of finding out to what she had been condemned and how long the sentence would be.

On the other hand, if she kept her head and took advantage of every little thing in her favour, she might be able to counter Greg's terms with a few of her own. Yes, that was what she must do—be cool, calm and unaffected by emotion. Perhaps she could trample her love underfoot, stamp down on it hard so that it would die and not hurt her any more.

CHAPTER THREE

GREG'S voice came over the wire, deep and harsh. 'Alex, I've been waiting for your call.'

'You're pretty sure of yourself!' She had been intending to say it under her breath, but it came out as a perfectly intelligible mutter.

He laughed and it set her teeth on edge, 'Oh, I knew your little sister would come flying to you to be rescued.'

Alex was in no mood for niceties or even middling good manners. 'What do you want?' she demanded.

'Simple! I want you to come round here straight away. It's the same flat we chose together before we were married.' He sounded amused. 'I'm sure you remember it.'

'I can't come straight away.' She was surly. 'I've only just come in and I need to shower and change, you'll have to give me a couple of hours at least.'

'Two hours, then,' he agreed, 'and wear your wedding ring, please. I noticed it was missing last night.'

'I wore that ring for three weeks precisely,' Alex hissed at the mouthpiece of the phone, becoming more angry than frightened. 'I took it off the night you left, and a little while later I was out for a walk and I dropped it in the river off Vauxhall Bridge.'

'Very wasteful,' was his comment. 'But never mind, I'll get you another, there's plenty of time and the shops are still open. And while I'm about it, I might just as well come and fetch you.'

Alex glared at the mouthpiece and enunciated carefully so that there would be no mistake about her meaning, 'I-do-not-want-another-one! And I don't want you to fetch me either, I'm quite capable of crossing London by myself. I'm quite a big girl now!'

'But you must have another one—think of how embarrassing it could be.' By closing her eyes, she could see his face and imagine the jeering look which would be curving his mouth. 'A wife without a wedding ring!' He was playing some game with her and evidently enjoying every moment of it. 'People, Lucy's mother-in-law for instance, would take a very dim view of such behaviour. She'd be rigid with disapproval.'

'Lucy's future mother-in-law,' she corrected him.

'She won't be, not unless you're ready to leave when I arrive to pick you up,' Greg chuckled. 'Two hours, you said—I'll be there at five sharp. Get your skates on, Alex.'

'And you *do* know her, Robert's mother I mean?'

'Of course,' he was bland. 'It was just as she told your sister, my parents used to have a house in St John's Wood when I was younger and the lady in question used to live next door. I thought I remembered young Robert last evening, he still has the same stodgy, earnest look. What is he now, a civil servant?'

'An optician.' Alex was brief. 'Fancy you not knowing that, or is your memory slipping?'

'I've a very good memory.' His tones became dulcet.

'Bully for you!' she spat the words as she hung up. He was right about his memory—it was more than good, it was phenomenal. If he'd seen it, heard it or read it, he remembered it.

Two hours was plenty of time and she had decided that she wasn't pulling out any stops in the matter of dress. She showered and changed into the best of her working suits, a prim affair in clerical grey, made do with the minimum of make-up and managed to screw her hair back into its short ponytail. Five o'clock was a good time, it would mean that she left the house before Ermine returned to it, so there would be no explanations as to where she was going. Just to be on the safe side, she scribbled a very brief note which gave nothing away—'Gone out. Ring if you want me'—and she added the number from the idiot board.

Before she left the flat, she hunted around in one of the small drawers of her dressing table and brought out a key. It was attached to a ring which held a minute furry bear, and her fingers lingered tenderly on the little mascot. Then she pulled herself together, wiped the sentimental expression from her face and stuffed both key and bear into her handbag. It hadn't brought her much in the way of luck.

Greg was waiting for her at the top of the area steps, leaning negligently against the railings. 'On time!' he marvelled, and his eyes ran over her disparagingly. Out of the corner of her eyes Alex watched a frown gather on his brow, then he shrugged and opened the door of the car for her, dismissing whatever had displeased him until a more opportune moment. Alex allowed a small smile to touch her mouth. Greg had always hated her in grey; let him hate! And she sat silent as he piloted the car back to Bayswater, weaving through the rush hour traffic as easily as though the monstrous thing was no bigger than a Mini.

It was a nice flat, and she recalled her delight when they had found it and the hard work she had put into the plans she had made for it. She had been going to furnish it with just the right things and had hunted high and low for pieces which would look right and for curtain fabrics that would blend. But that had been when there were stars in her eyes, when she had thought that love would go on for ever. A bitter little smile touched her lips as he let her in through the door—her love had gone on, but Greg's was of a different kind, it hadn't possessed him completely as hers had done. He had fallen at the first hurdle.

She noticed that the place looked very much as she had planned and that everything was fresh and well cared for. It must cost a mint to keep the place and to keep it in this condition—but then Greg had no money worries and he certainly wouldn't bother about a tiny detail like the enormous cost of a flat he only used a couple of times a year. Money meant very little to him. The books he wrote, the digs he supervised and his lecturing—these were merely his playthings, he didn't do them for the money; he didn't have to. His mother had left him an adequate income that made him a wealthy, hardworking libertine. Alex snorted softly with disgust. Without that money, he would have been a hard-up, hardworking libertine. She wondered where he found time for the 'libertine' bit.

'Do you still have your key, Alex? I remember you put it on a ring with a silly little teddy bear, you said it was your lucky piece.'

'It didn't bring me much luck.' She should have known he would remember, but she wasn't going to admit that she still had it.

His eyes slid over her, taking in the severe-looking suit, the creamy blouse with the little black bow at the rather mannish collar, her grey silk stockings and the low-heeled black patent pumps.

'Mmm, much thinner than you used to be—and what does all this mean?' He was walking her down the hall and into the lounge and he gestured briefly at her clothing. 'You used not to be so badly dressed. Am I supposed to be put off?'

Alex didn't bother to answer the question, other things were more important. 'What exactly have you been hatching up with Lucy?' she demanded, 'and why didn't you tell me about it last night?'

'Why should I tell you? That was something Lucy had to do for herself. I don't mind helping her out of a mess, but I told the little fool, she'd have to make her own explanations.' His grey eyes looked down at her with no expression in them. 'To be blunt, she ran off at the mouth in order to make a good impression, a silly thing to do with somebody like Robert Latchford's mother, she might have known . . .'

'She's very young and very much in love,' Alex

protested. 'And she didn't tell any lies. I expect that if I'd gone to see the lady and explained. . . .'

'. . . Then you don't know Mrs Latchford,' he interrupted. 'She's the sort of woman who makes instant judgments and sticks to them through thick and thin. What's more, she holds the purse strings very tightly, and as far as her son is concerned, I should imagine her word is law.'

Alex shook her head, 'If Lucy and Robert are in love, they should be given a chance . . .'

'. . . And isn't that what Lucy's asking of you?' Greg stretched himself lazily in a chair opposite her, leaning back and looking thoroughly at ease. 'Dear little Lucy! As I said, your Achilles heel, my dear. Would you care for a glass of sherry before dinner?'

'No, thank you.' Her manner was as prim as her hair, her face and her clothes. 'I'm not staying for dinner, I—er—have another appointment.' As she said it, she realised that it was so faint a hope as to be no hope at all, and her fingers crisped on the handle of her bag as she remained standing. One of Greg's dark eyebrows flew up as he gestured her towards the chesterfield couch.

'Sit down, my dear.' His voice had lost its laziness and was now soft and menacing. 'Sit down and listen while I tell you what you *are* going to do. You're going to drink a glass of sherry, then you will join me for dinner, which is all ready for us in the kitchen. After dinner, we'll have a little chat about the future, and then we shall go to bed.'

'No!' It came out explosively before she could stop it and she took a deep breath. 'I can't do that—Ermine will start worrying where I am and I don't know if Lucy's coming home tonight ... In any case, I can't stay, I haven't brought anything with me.' The last sentence came out with a spark of defiant triumph.

'So I noticed.' Greg dealt with the clothing problem first and in a very terse way. 'My sweet, if what you're wearing is a sample of your present wardrobe,' and he waved a denigratory hand at her suit, 'I'm very glad you didn't bring any more of it and you needn't bother to send for the rest. That outfit makes you look sexless—what do you wear underneath it, white cotton interlock?'

Alex flushed with embarrassment. For three years, her underwear had been her own business, and she was unused to discussing it—and certainly not with Greg. He was the sort of man who made the mention of bras and panties sound almost immoral; he would grin and look speculatively at the areas they covered.

'There are quite a few of your things here,' he broke in on her thoughts. 'You left quite a lot of stuff in the old flat—I had it all brought round here ...'

'It will all be years out of date,' she reminded him tartly.

'So fussy!' His smile glimmered across at her and she felt the old familiar knot tighten in her stomach. 'But out of date or not, you had a better dress sense then than now,' he dismissed her objections airily. 'In any case, you only want something to sleep in.'

Alex shrugged to cover her dismay. 'I'm not sleeping with you,' she told him defiantly, but even this last-ditch stand was denied her. He was gently reproving.

'You mustn't be so forward, my love. You must wait till you're asked!'

'And Ermine and Lucy?' She made a quick recovery, although his humiliating reply had bitten deep. 'I'll probably have to go back and tell Ermine. If Lucy's not there, it's no use ringing; the phone's in the basement flat and Ermine wouldn't hear it.'

'Then let her sweat a bit,' he said crudely. 'Or you could ring one of the other tenants and get them to pass on a message. Stop bothering about it, wait until after dinner—and by the way,' he extracted a small box from his pocket, 'your new wedding ring; as near as I could get to the original and with the same inscription inside, or didn't you bother to examine the old one before you threw it away?'

'No, I didn't. I told you, I took it off and dropped it in the river. There was hardly a splash.'

'Perhaps you'd like to look at this one?' He held it out to her, 'And don't try throwing this one away. The windows are double-glazed, there's no fire and it will be on your finger before you can get to the waste disposal unit in the kitchen. Look at it, Alex!' It was a command.

She turned the chased gold circlet in her fingers. It was thick, wide and very heavy, but the inscription defeated her. It was too small to read without her glasses and although she squinted at it from several angles, she couldn't make it out.

'I'd need my spectacles and I didn't bring them with me,' she explained. 'So it's just an inscription as far as I'm concerned. One wedding ring suitably inscribed with date and initials, I suppose—it means nothing to me,' and she tossed the ring down on to the onyx top of the occasional table where it rang metallically for a few seconds until it settled into silence.

The speed at which Greg moved shocked her into immobility. One second he was lounging in the chair opposite her, and the next he was by her side and the ring was being pushed on to her finger. It was a tight fit and she yelped with pain as he forced it brutally over her knuckle.

'A good fit.' He turned the ring one way and the other, testing for looseness. 'I don't think you'll get that one off in a hurry, Mrs Mallus—and now you'll never know what the inscription was. Ask me some time and I might tell you.'

Alex nursed her bruised finger and tried to keep tears of pain out of her eyes as she asked, 'And my sister and Ermine?'

But his hand was under her elbow, pulling her to her feet. 'After dinner,' he assured her. 'Come on.'

Alex found she was hungry after all; she also discovered that she'd drunk the sherry. It had been pale and very dry and it must have given her an appetite, something which she'd lost since her bout of influenza. The cold consommé was delicious, the lobster thermidor superb, but she'd skipped the sweet in favour of several cups of well sweetened coffee in the hope that they would drive away some of the muzziness induced by two glasses of a superior Graves which had slid down her throat almost unnoticed.

She wondered who had done the cooking. The

meal hadn't all come out of tins— the consommé could have done, but she had yet to see the tin which would hold that much lobster. Of one thing she was certain, Greg hadn't cooked it! In a kitchen, he was a disaster looking for somewhere to happen, he couldn't boil an egg properly, and it wasn't that he didn't know how. She remembered the old days when he'd tried, something always went wrong; but she wasn't going to ask a question which might imply that she was interested or that she had any intention of staying.

When the meal was finished, Greg escorted her back to the lounge, remarking that she could turn the heating up if she wasn't warm enough, and then he left her to her own devices. She heard him go into the small room which he used as a sort of office and she sank back on to the chesterfield with a sigh which was almost contented. The lounge was delightfully warm, the lights were dimmed and the whole flat was a haven of peace. It was hard to realise she was here against her will. She hitched another cushion under her head and her eyes drifted shut.

When Greg came back into the room, she opened one eye and surveyed him drowsily. 'What about Ermine and Lucy?' she queried.

'No bother,' he stood over her, looking down at her face with a satisfied expression. 'I've just phoned your number and Lucy answered. Apparently, she decided to come home after all. I told her you were staying here and that she'd nothing further to worry about, that we were going to give the impression of a happily wedded couple. Little Lucy abandoned you to the lion, my dear and without a single qualm. How does it feel to be a martyr?' He selected a cigarette from the box on the table, lit it and looked at her through the smoke. 'But you always liked being a martyr, didn't you? It's your favourite occupation, tying yourself to a stake and handing somebody the matches to light your funeral fire.'

Viewed from this angle, his resemblance to the Demon King of pantomime was very marked. The two streaks of white in his hair looked like incipient horns and Alex stirred herself out of her lethargy.

'I don't suppose you gave her a chance to say anything,' she accused him crossly. 'You've always been the same. It's only what *you* say and think that's important; you never listen to anybody!'

'On the contrary, my dear wife; I gave your little sister ample opportunity to say anything she pleased, but when I told her you wouldn't be coming back to Kensington, her reply was "Oh, good!" Whatever have you done to deserve such sisterly devotion? As for your dear aunt, that little lady is quite capable of looking after herself. She doesn't need you to tuck her up and kiss her goodnight.'

'And you, I suppose, do?'

'Mmm.' He sat down in the chair opposite, leaning back and crossing his long legs, studying her through the smoke of his cigarette. 'Apart from the fact that you're my wife and your place is here, I've a lot of writing to do. I spent my last summer vacation at a dig outside Gloucester, the remains of a very fine villa. We opened most of it and it gives a marvellous picture of Roman colonial life in the last years of the Empire. I used it in my television series as an example of how the Romans lived in an outpost of the empire. The mosaics alone were quite unique, two of the floors were complete and had been hardly damaged and there were sufficient remains of a third to be able to reconstruct it. Now we have to produce a book of the series, so I'll get my notes together and the photographs that were taken . . .'

'Oh!' Alex gasped with a mingled feeling of disappointment and exasperation. 'So that's why you've brought me here, is it? You're writing again and you need a typist! One you can bawl at and who won't answer back. You're despicable!'

'What's the matter?' Greg could be uncannily acute at times. 'Are you disappointed that I'm not going to rape you?'

'No, I'm relieved,' she told him sweetly. 'But you've set another problem and I'm afraid this time, you'll have to let me go home. I can't work without my spectacles and I didn't bring them with me. You see, I thought this was going to be a seduction scene and I didn't want to spoil it for you.'

'Then you should have brought a black chiffon nightie.' She thought he might be laughing at her. 'You used to look good in black, filmy things; you glimmered through them.'

This sort of conversation was getting her nowhere—well, nowhere she wanted to go—so she changed the subject. 'You realise that as soon as Lucy gets married, you can't keep me here any longer.'

'One step at a time, Alex,' he waved it aside.

'Lucy told me she was looking forward to a long, romantic engagement, she mentioned six months, so that gives us plenty of time, and you can forget about your spectacles for a while, you're not fit to be working yet.' He smiled at her and she moaned silently. Greg had always had that heart-stopping smile. He didn't use it very much, mainly, she thought bitterly, when he wanted to get his own way—and it didn't stop her heart, it accelerated it until she became breathless. 'We'll collect them for you on Monday morning, how will that suit? And how long have you been wearing them?'

'About two years.' Alex closed her eyes so that she didn't have to see him and leaned back against the cushions. Her heartbeat steadied and her breathing became normal and she was aware of a lethargy stealing over her, so that she could hardly find the energy to open her eyes. 'The house conversion cost a lot and I had to raise a mortgage—the repayments were so high that until the flats were let I had to take in other work, typing manuscripts, theses and things like that at home in the evenings. I started to get headaches, I thought it was migraine, but spectacles soon cured it. But I'm always leaving them somewhere or forgetting to take them with me. . . .' The last words faded into incoherency as her head slid down among the cushions and she slept.

When she woke, it was late afternoon; she stirred in the soft bed and stared around the unfamiliar room, trying to remember where she was. Then memory came rushing back and her eyes started to identify small articles—the silver-backed brushes and hand-mirror which had been part of Greg's wedding present to her, the silver-topped crystal bits and bobs which she had found in an antique shop and had brought home in triumph to wash and polish. There was the little bedside clock as well, a gilt wreath upheld by the tail of a classical dolphin mounted on an agate plinth.

It was ticking softly and her eyes went to the enamel dial within the wreath. It said five o'clock, but that was impossible, so she checked against her watch which had stopped at half past ten and was therefore useless. But the quality of the daylight told her it wasn't morning, the shadows were gathering, and she struggled up in the bed, only to slide down again swiftly as she discovered her nudity.

She hadn't put herself to bed in this state and then she remembered, she hadn't put herself to bed at all. Greg had done this, and hot colour flooded all over her. She could recall discussing a similar situation with Lucy one morning when she had found her sister asleep, covered by the duvet and nothing else.

'You shouldn't,' she had reprimanded weakly.

'Why not?' and Lucy had cocked an impertinent eyebrow.

Alex had dredged her mind for a reason which didn't sound too stuffy. 'Suppose there was a fire?'

And Lucy had grinned at her. 'If there was, who do you think our gallant firemen would rescue first, me or Aunty in her pintucked cotton? You'd be their second choice,' she had added generously, and Alex had retired, defeated from the encounter.

But it was the knowledge of who had stripped

her that made her blush, and out of the corner of her eye she spotted a slither of oyster-coloured, lace-trimmed silk. That brought back memories as well. It had been bought specially for her honeymoon and at Lucy's instigation. Her sister had dismissed anything not made of silk as being reminiscent of carbolic soap and toothpaste, and Alex had spent far more than she could afford on pure silk, dripping with lace, and had felt sybaritic, erotic and faintly guilty.

Unbidden, the memory came of Greg when he had seen her in it. He had chuckled and quoted somebody, 'Armour against pleasure and a cobweb against danger' as he had slipped open the tiny buttons that fastened it and slipped it from her shoulders until it fell around her feet in a glimmering pool. Desperately, Alex turned her face into the pillow, trying to blot out the memory. It was all so long ago, it was in the past, it had nothing to do with the person she was now. She had got over that, the wanting, the longing. It had all ended in a nightmare almost before it had begun—she looked down at the nightgown—but that he should have kept it for so long!

Swiftly she slid herself into the garment and was just fastening the buttons when the door opened to admit her husband. It was as if she had conjured him up just by thinking about him.

'Feeling better?' He made it sound as though he was really interested.

'Thank you, yes.' She now had a firm hold on herself and her voice was noncommittal. 'But there was no need for you to have put me to bed, you could have wakened me.'

'Wakened you!' He gave a snort of laughter. 'You were like something dead, and you wouldn't have been comfortable sleeping in your clothes. Undressing you was easy, if disappointing, you're little more than a skeleton, but getting you into a nightie defeated me, so I left well alone.'

The hot colour in her cheeks revealed her thoughts as though she had spoken them aloud, and his smile became satanic. 'No, I didn't!' and then the smile disappeared and he became enigmatic while she registered that he still had those incredibly long eyelashes and that they and his heavy lids masked his eyes so that she couldn't tell what he was thinking. 'I told you,' he continued smoothly, although there was a wry twist to his mouth. 'You'll wait until you're asked, although last night, I came up with a much better idea. You'll wait until *you* ask *me*. Yes, that's much more like it—you'll beg, Alexandra.'

'Then we'll both wait a long, long time,' she countered swiftly, and turned her back on him.

A hand on her shoulder brought her back to face him. 'No, not so long,' Greg murmured. 'I made myself a promise, but I think, just for this once, I'll break it. You remember what it was like? Yes, you do,' as she shook her head. 'And you enjoyed it as much as I did, because under all that puritanical virtue, there's a little wanton trying to get out. You'll want me again, my sweet, and when you do,' his head jerked to the communicating door, 'I sleep in there and the key's on your side. You're welcome at any time, all you have to do is turn that key, walk in and ask me nicely!'

Alex moved her head to avoid him, but her face was brought back to his with a steely finger and thumb at her chin so that she closed her eyes and tried to be coldly unaffected as his mouth found hers. Just for a second she succeeded, and then something which had been bottled up inside her for three years burst. It didn't matter any more that there had been other women, that Greg had told her ages ago that he never refused an offer. With a gulp of despair, she felt her lips part under his and her hand rose to fondle his shoulder.

'Mmm,' he murmured as he raised his head to look down at her drowsy eyes and red, inviting mouth. 'Not long at all! Control yourself, Alex— or have you got over your hang-up about making love in the daytime? I'll bring you a nice cup of tea.'

When the door closed behind him, Alex rolled over and buried her hot face in the pillow. It hadn't happened, she had imagined it! She couldn't have behaved in that way, slopping all over a tall, dark, handsome charmer with a doubtful reputation, even if he was her husband and she loved him. But she knew she had, and there had to be a reason, an excuse. Finally she solved it. She was a perfectly normal woman and she had just passed three years in a far from normal way. She had kept well away from men and immersed herself in what remained of her family. She hadn't been kissed, not once! It was no wonder that she'd just gone overboard with an almighty splash; and Greg was an expert, he knew very well how to wake her up. He'd been keeping in practice while she went her lonely way. In other words, she wasn't to blame at all!

So that when he returned with the promised cup of tea, she could face him with a degree of self-confidence and a tight, shuttered half smile as she took the cup from his hand.

'Thank you.' It wasn't her normal voice, it sounded forced and a bit squeaky even to her own ears, but Greg wasn't in a noticing mood, he had other things on his mind.

'Dinner,' he said in quite an ordinary voice as though that kiss had never happened. 'What do you fancy? Just say the word and I'll get it for you—and don't say you're not hungry, because you've been asleep for nearly fifteen hours—you must be hungry by now.'

'You cooking!' Her lip lifted in a delicate sneer. 'The heaven's will open on that day. You were always hopeless, you'd burn water!'

'Which is why I don't do it, Madam Disdain,' he retorted. 'There's a good restaurant in the next street and they do outside meals. They send up whatever I order in containers—so what do you fancy?' He gave her another assessing look. 'Steak, I think—you obviously need building up.'

'Order what you like,' she said ungraciously. 'If I don't like it, I don't have to eat it.'

'Yes, you do.' He sat down on the side of the bed with a thump so that the tea slopped over into the saucer. 'You're much too thin and I don't fancy skeletal women, although I'll make an exception in your case. I'll order for half past seven, so there's time for you to get a shower and slip into a robe before the food arrives. And by the way, I've been in touch with your sister, she's going to pack up your stuff and bring it over this evening. She said we could expect her about nine.'

'I could have got my things myself,' Alex muttered. 'There wasn't any need to drag Lucy all this way.'

'Nobody's being dragged anywhere.' Greg shook his head at her. 'Today's Saturday and Lucy's staying in her boy-friend's house for the weekend. This flat's on her way.'

'But she can't!' Alex forced the empty cup on him and made to slide out of the bed. 'Ermine will be alone. Please, Greg, you *must* let me go back, you know how nervous she is.'

'Of what?' He was unimpressed and his eyebrows flew up to give him a look of Mephistopheles, as though he was enjoying the thought of Ermine being alone and nervous. 'Nobody's going to break in and assault her!' And carrying the cup and saucer with exaggerated caution, he went out, closing the door behind him with a thud of finality.

Alex slipped out of bed and sped along to the bathroom to admire the improvements made there. The last time she had seen it, it had been white and strictly utilitarian. Now it boasted a plum-coloured suite with a separate shower and pale turquoise tiles everywhere. There wasn't much in the way of feminine toiletries on the shelves, and she showered with the contents of a plastic bottle whose label bore the picture of a surfer on incredibly big and blue waves, hoping that it wouldn't clash with the eau de toilette spray in her handbag.

Back in the bedroom, wrapped in an enormous bathsheet and smelling nicely of 'Marque Noir', she riffled through the clothes in the wardrobe. Of her grey suit there was no sign, and the remainder of the clothing hung on her limply. She tried the only undateable dress, a classic shirtwaister in striped silk, and decided that if it was a morale-booster she required, she wouldn't get much help from this dress. It was too everything—too long, too wide, and the neckline accentuated the thinness of her neck and the way her collarbones protruded.

Greg was right, she had lost too much weight, but it had gone so slowly over three years that she hadn't noticed. With an air of determination she reclothed herself in the nightgown, found the matching negligee and belted it firmly about her waist before she made her way to the kitchen where Greg was dealing with a pile of metal containers. Whatever was inside them smelled very good and Alex went willingly to lay up the table in the dining area, her mouth watering with pleasurable anticipation.

The dinner was good, but Alex found herself eating it in frozen silence. If she hadn't been so hungry, she would have thrown her plate at him as he sat opposite her in a similar silence. Several times he looked as though he was going to say something, but on these occasions she lowered her eyes to her plate and chewed stolidly. Greg seemed to find this offputting and after his first cup of coffee, he rose abruptly and almost stamped out of the kitchen.

Alex watched his retreating back, and when the

door closed behind him, she gave the panels a spiteful smile and poured herself another cup of coffee.

CHAPTER FOUR

AT a quarter to nine, when the kitchen was once again tidy and neat, with the containers stacked ready awaiting collection, the doorbell rang, and Alex hurried to answer it despite the fact that she was still wearing the nightgown and negligee. This would be Lucy, so dress wasn't important. Her sister stood outside, laden with two untidily packed suitcases and a couple of bulging plastic carrier bags.

'Hello, Alex.' Lucy took one step into the hallway and dropped her burdens. The carrier bags disgorged their contents on to the floor and the locks of one of the suitcases sprang open, but Lucy ignored such minor details. She stepped over the clutter and stood peering round, admiring a couple of Japanese prints which decorated the austere walls. 'This is a bit swish, isn't it? What's the rest of it like?'

'It matches the hall,' Alex said dryly. 'What's known, I believe, as an elegant abode. Come into the kitchen, we can talk there.'

Her sister sighed. 'I might have known! My only sister goes up in the world, gets to live in an elegant abode and when I visit her, she asks me into the kitchen! What's the matter, is Greg in the lounge?'

Alex shrugged. 'I don't know, but in the kitchen we can make coffee, so come on,' and she led the way down the small hall. Once in the kitchen, Lucy flung herself into a chair and smiled seraphically.

'I'm glad you're happy, Alex.'

Alex opened her mouth to deny any form of happiness and then shut it again quickly. If Lucy thought she was happy, well and good! She watched her sister resting plump white arms on the table, her chin cupped in her hands as her eyes wandered over the appointments. She nodded appreciation of the dishwasher, the micro-wave oven and all the rest of the labour-saving devices; apparently Lucy thought that a couple of thousand pounds' worth of electrical impedimenta was all that was necessary for complete bliss!

The coffee machine gurgled its load into the waiting jug and Alex fetched big stoneware mugs, waiting for some sign of thanks for the sacrifice she was making. She waited in vain. Lucy was brimming with good tidings and she obviously thought Alex was doing pretty well.

'I've had this marvellous idea!' Lucy's eyes were sparkling. 'I'm going to move in with a couple of girls I know, sharing a small flat, and then I can let ours. The rent will be extra income for me and I'm going to need every penny I can lay my hands on. Getting married is a very expensive business, I need so much. I was thinking, though, if Greg would give me away and you'd do the reception thing—I mean I could leave it all to you, the food, the drinks, the cake and champagne, you know. But don't you think it's a good idea about the flat? Sheer inspiration, I thought!'

'But wouldn't you like to keep it?' Alex

demurred, although she knew she was wasting her breath. 'I thought you and Robert might like . . .' It was only an excuse to cover the possibility that as soon as Lucy was safely married she, Alex, might need the flat herself.

'Me and Robert? Oh no,' Lucy registered amazement that her sister could think such a thing. 'I wouldn't like to begin our married life there. It's so old-fashioned and quiet, I'd have nobody to talk to. I want us to have a nice modern house on a modern estate—somewhere with young wives of my own age group. Hounslow, I think, but we haven't decided yet.' She gave a little giggle and became conspiratorial. 'Robert's mother thinks we're going to share her house, but I've told him that's not on! I'm not starting my married life by living with my mother-in-law. But you haven't said—don't you think it's a good idea, me moving in with friends? I have to live somewhere and I don't fancy being in the flat on my own, there's too much housework. Besides, I'm fed up with Aunty, she gets on my nerves.'

'You've hardly given me a chance to say anything,' Alex had been listening with only half an ear, 'but I think it's probably the best thing you can do—move in with some girls, I mean, but don't bother about finding a tenant for the flat; I'll put it in the hands of the solicitor.'

'But then I won't get the rent, and I need it,' Lucy said mutinously.

'Sorry,' Alex shrugged, 'but that's one thing you can't have. There are the mortgage repayments and I shan't be working so I'll have no income . . . When are you getting married?'

'Robert says——' and Lucy went on at length to explain how her new fiancé had gone into it very thoroughly; as became a dependable and thoughtful husband-to-be. He had decided that October was the most financially suitable time and the most beneficial, 'And at that time of the year,' Lucy enthused, 'there'll be lots of cut-price holidays abroad, so we can have a gorgeous honeymoon for lots less than we'd pay in June. We save money all round!'

Alex nodded again while she wilted inwardly. It was now March and it meant that she would be tied to this ghastly situation for the next six months. She gave a mental shrug—it couldn't be cured, it would have to be endured, and by chance, it was just the period she would use when she wrote her story of a second try at marriage. She twisted her face into the semblance of a smile. 'Lovely—I'm very glad for you.'

'And I'm glad for you,' Lucy said generously. 'You seem to be settling down, and I hope that this time you'll stick it out and make a go of it.' Her young face became serious and she pursed her mouth so that, for a second, she looked very like Ermine about to deliver a lecture. 'This is where you belong, you know—a wife's place is with her husband, that's what Robert says, and I agree with him. I wouldn't let anything separate us,' and she was off, burbling happily about Robert's birthday party which was now to be their engagement party and promising invitations during the next week or so.

When the door closed behind her, Alex turned back and began, on her hands and knees, to stuff things back into carrier bags while depression settled on her about a foot thick. It was thus that Greg found her when he came out of his study—and he stood looking down at her without pity.

'From the expression on your face, your little sister has been both insensitive and unco-operative,' he hazarded. 'It's your own fault, my dear—your parents must have spoiled her and when they died, you carried on the good work.'

'You don't understand.' Alex scrambled to her feet, a shoe swinging from either hand. 'Lucy lost so much. At least I had Mummy and Daddy until I was seventeen, but Lucy was only a child at the time, so I had to make it up to her. She'd been deprived of their love and care just when she needed it most . . .'

'. . . Go, on!' he jeered at her. 'A few more heartrending speeches like that and you'll have me in tears!'

Her hand rose and a shoe whizzed past his ear. 'I had to make it up to her, you arrogant pig!' Her voice choked with temper and the second shoe followed the first. Greg caught it adroitly.

'And what's this mess?' He regarded the scatter on the floor with distaste. 'Your clothes?' He looked at the shoe in his hand, black, low-heeled and very plain. 'Why did you bother?' With the toe of his shoe he pushed up the lid of the case with the sprung locks, grimaced at its contents and let it fall again on the ill-packed contents. 'Mary Poppins in person! Never mind, we'll get rid of the worst, all that ghastly grey and starch and you can start all over again.'

His fingers grasped her elbow, preventing her

from getting on with her tidying up and he steered her into the lounge to push her down on to the couch with none too gentle a hand.

'We'll get rid of nothing,' she glared up at him. 'They're *my* clothes, I bought them, I like them . . .'

'. . . And I have to look at them, and I don't like what I see. All that grey doesn't suit you.' Greg dropped down beside her on the couch and slanted a comprehensive glance at her. 'Just at present, you don't look too bad; that négligé thing does something for you, it makes you look like an abandoned hussy. Mmm, I wonder how far I'd have to push you before you started begging.'

'You'd be wasting your time,' she threatened, although there was a tight feeling about her chest as though there wasn't enough air in the room for both of them. The palms of her hands were damp and there was a clamouring ache in the pit of her stomach. She turned her head away from him and concentrated on a large crystal ashtray; what she was going to do wouldn't be very brave, but she wasn't feeling brave, she was feeling weak and cowardly. 'I'm tired,' she muttered, 'I think I'll go to bed.' and she fled from the room pursued by his jeering laughter.

Sunday was a day of rest, but on Monday morning, Greg started his take over plan in earnest, organising her with a brutal, ruthless efficiency so that all she had to say was 'Yes', 'No' and 'Thank you'. He donated her good suit, her shirt blouses, all her grey stockings and several pairs of sensible shoes to a woman who was collecting for a local Boy Scouts' jumble sale, and his management didn't stop there. A telephone call to the agency that employed her and Alex joined the ranks of the unemployed.

She wasn't in the least grateful for the organisation—to her, it was a diabolical liberty taken with her personal freedom, and she choked on wrath and went about the flat looking as though there was a bad smell under her nose, but apart from that, there was nothing she could do. She kept her nose elevated and her mouth shut, but there were hectic spots of colour in her cheeks and a pronounced glitter in her eyes. Greg looked at her approvingly.

'That's the first sign of animation I've seen in you,' he commented as she studiously avoided his eyes, concentrating all her attention on the herb omelettes which she was making for lunch.

'I don't have an extensive wardrobe,' her tone was flat and uncompromising, 'and I can't afford to give away half of it,' she looked down at the skirt and tee-shirt she was wearing with distaste. 'I don't feel right. I don't want . . .'

'This afternoon,' he said blandly, 'we'll go out and buy you some new stuff; something a bit more becoming.'

'I do not want you to buy me anything,' she told him loftily.

'Alexandra,' his voice was soft with a threat underlying the softness, 'I thought I'd made it plain to you—what you want doesn't interest me in the slightest. You called the tune three years ago and I let you have your way, now it's my turn.'

She blinked with shock, thought up several stinging retorts and then decided against saying any of them. It wasn't any good getting into a verbal battle with Greg; he had one great advantage—he didn't care what he said or who he hurt. She took refuge in a cool, over-polite remoteness and forced her face into a bland acceptance of the inevitable.

'But how are you going to explain it away?—us being back together again, I mean. Aren't some people going to start asking awkward questions?'

'Explain?' He looked at her as if he was surprised she should have thought such a thing. 'We don't explain, why should we? Our private life is very much our own business, it doesn't concern anybody else. If you look at it that way and behave accordingly, you'll find there won't be any questions asked.'

'Then I'm afraid I shall have to leave it to you.' A small, tight smile curved her mouth. 'You can carry it off in your usual high-handed manner and I'll smile as though I think you always know best and that, as far as I'm concerned, you're the only man in the world.'

'Have there been any other men?' he demanded peremptorily, and Alex hung on to her cool remoteness with difficulty. She would have liked to yell 'dozens', but she wasn't much good at lies, she wasn't sure she'd be able to carry it off, so she stuck to the truth. 'None. You put me off!' She glanced at her watch and checked it against the clock. 'If there's shopping to do, hadn't we better have lunch and then go and do it?'

On Tuesday afternoon, just after five-thirty, Alex descended from a cab outside the Kensington house laden with parcels. Before she mounted the steps to the main door, she checked her remaining money and was pleased to find that even allowing for the amount she'd spent on cosmetics, bathroom stuff—she'd come to the end of the 'surfer' bath gel—and after she'd paid out quite a large sum for a small bottle of her favourite perfume, she still had nearly twenty pounds. It wasn't a fortune, but it was all her own, and she had to make it last quite a long time.

Greg had opened an account for her at one of the big stores and although she had sworn to herself that she wouldn't use it, she had fallen for the temptation of pure silk underwear and several other expensive trifles which she hadn't been able to resist. The underwear would be gorgeous beneath the dress which Greg had forced her to buy for Lucy's engagement party.

It was a drifting thing in green chiffon which she had loved on sight and then hated because of the price tag. She had tried it on and he had nodded with satisfaction, which had made her hate it more, so that she was quite pleased when it had been pointed out to her that it was marginally too long. Alex had looked at her husband with a triumphant gleam in her eyes, but her triumph was shortlived. Greg had agreed with the saleswoman and had said 'shorten it' without another glance at his wife.

'It's a waste of money,' she had protested when they had returned home. 'It's not the sort of dress I can wear any old time. It's an 'occasion' dress.'

'And doesn't your sister's engagement party come under that heading?'

Alex had tilted her chin. 'I don't think it warrants a Paris model.'

'My dear,' Greg had sounded weary of their continual bickering, 'we are going to this party because Lucy wants us there, and you are *not* going in that Jane Eyre outfit you were wearing when I met you on Thursday evening. You might get some sort of kick out of looking prim and governessy, but it won't go down very well with Lucy's prospective mother-in-law. You've never met her, remember—you've a treat in store.'

'How?'

'Mrs Latchford's a snob.' If anything, he sounded more weary. 'She always was, and she doesn't seem to have changed for the better. You'll probably disagree with me, you usually do, but the woman's found a presentable sister for her son's fiancée and she's going to make the most of it. She's expecting me in a starched shirt and a dinner jacket and because she knows I can afford it, she'll expect you in something breathtaking. Anything less than a Paris model and she'll feel slighted, so you see you owe it to Lucy—and for pity's sake, don't wear your hair in that ghastly pony tail!'

Alex had maintained her cool, although it was becoming increasingly difficult. She was totally dependent on her husband, a state of affairs which filled her with alarm, and then there was the mortgage . . .

All these thoughts were flickering through her mind as she climbed the steps to the front door, inserted her key and went through to Ermine's private door, where she knocked and prepared to wait, but her aunt was opening the door almost before Alex had released the small brass knocker which Ermine had preferred to the usual bellpush. Alex's eyebrows rose a fraction—Lucy was right, then, Ermine kept a close watch on what went on in the street below her windows.

She struggled through the doorway and dropped her packages just inside the sitting room door, noting with surprise that the table was laid for tea. Ermine caught the look.

'I've been expecting you,' she smiled. 'I've a kind of sixth sense where you're concerned, Alex. I knew you'd come at the first opportunity. I couldn't be sure when it would be—I knew you'd have difficulty getting away on your own and I knew he wouldn't come here—he's too ashamed to face me.'

'Greg's my husband, not my jailer,' Alex pointed out gently, forbearing to enlighten her aunt to the fact that Greg didn't know what shame was! She sank into a chair and lifted the corner of one of the thinly cut triangular sandwiches. 'Egg and cress, how lovely!'

'Mmm.' Ermine busied herself with the teapot. 'I had everything ready, just in case you came, and the scones are fresh, I bought them today on the way home from the office.' She handed over a cup of tea. 'Why did you do it, Alex—go back to him, I mean? I don't think it was a very wise thing to do.'

Alex accepted the cup and stirred in sugar thoughtfully while she forced her face into a noncommittal expression. 'What's wise, my dear? He's my husband . . .

'But not the one I'd have chosen for you.' Ermine was faintly regretful. 'You're not eating, dear,' she pointed out, offering the sandwich plate.

Alex shook her head. 'I daren't. This isn't the old days, remember, when we made pigs of ourselves at teatime. Today I have to go back and have dinner with Greg at eight . . .'

'Then don't go,' Ermine said softly, almost under her breath. 'Stay here with me for the evening. He's not the man for you, Alex, I said so when you first brought him here before you were married. He's too aggressive for you, too crude and insensitive.'

Alex thought about that one. She thought of a number of adjectives to describe her husband—domineering, conceited, implacable, hurtful and a dozen or so others even less complimentary, but oddly enough, 'aggressive' wasn't one of them. 'Abrasive' perhaps—her lips curved into a reminiscent smile. Greg was like hard emery, he rubbed people down to fit in with his peculiar quirks. She carried the analogy a step further and chuckled to herself. Greg sandblasted!

'You think that's amusing?' Ermine poked a tendril of hair back into her neat hairdo. 'But I'm right, I know I am. I'm a very good judge of character and I'm sure you couldn't ever be happy with a man like that.'

'I didn't have much chance to find out.' Alex took another sip of tea. 'It didn't last long enough.'

'But you've gone back to him!' it was almost a wail. 'I don't know how you could—did he force you into it?'

Alex helped herself to a scone and bit into it deliberately; she couldn't speak with her mouth full and she needed time to think. Coming here this afternoon mightn't have been such a good idea after all. Ermine was asking the sixty-four-dollar question and Alex couldn't tell the truth.

She couldn't say 'Yes, he forced me. Lucy had been indiscreet and he offered a way out'—Lucy's verbal indiscretions were a byword and Ermine would seize on it. Lucy was Ermine's least favourite person.

'Force me?' She raised a haughty eyebrow over the rim of her cup. 'How could he do that? No, we thought we ought to give it another try.' She took Lucy's engagement period again, it was such a nice round figure, quite believable. 'Six months, we thought. We're both a bit older now and we ought to be able to be adult about it.'

Her aunt smiled sympathetically. 'You're too forgiving, dear—too gentle. In your place, I should feel unable to trust him again. I can't think why you didn't get a divorce, that would have been the simplest thing. You made a mistake and you paid bitterly for it, and he was the one who walked out! The least he could have done was to give you your freedom . . .'

Ermine's gentle monologue went on and Alex stopped listening well before the part where her aunt detailed all their sufferings—Lucy's wildness, the inconvenience while the house was being converted and the cramped conditions which they now suffered compared with the amount of living space available in the old days. She'd heard it all before, but this was the first time that the blame for every one of these pinpricking inconveniences had been laid at Greg's door. But it did remind her about her spectacles and she was just about to ask for them when Lucy slammed her way in. Ermine looked annoyed.

'Lucy, just listen to her! She can't do anything quietly. You spoiled that girl, Alex.'

'Just what Greg told me,' Alex grinned weakly. 'You two have that point in common—although it's about all you do share,' she added ruefully as running footsteps came along the corridor and Lucy burst into the room.

'You're nicked!' Her sister giggled at the surprise on Alex's face. 'I rang you after lunch, I wanted to ask a favour, but you weren't there. Greg said you'd gone shopping. I didn't expect to find you here, was it an arranged thing?'

'No,' now Alex could be serene, 'I called without any arrangements being made. I need my spectacles and I left them downstairs in the basement.'

'Nice to see you, though.' Lucy seized a sandwich, stuffed it in her mouth and spoke through the crumbs. 'It'll help brighten Aunty up, she's been going round in a haze of misery imagining you in the clutches of the monster!' She turned an enquiring glance on Ermine, who was looking tightlipped. 'What's the matter, Aunty dear, do you grudge me a sandwich? I'm too tired to make my own. And,' her eyes fell on the heap of parcels by the door, 'you've been shopping! What's the matter, isn't anybody talking to me?'

'We don't get a chance,' Alex grinned at her sister. 'You haven't stopped talking since you came in.'

Lucy grinned back and stuffed a scone into her

mouth before going to investigate the pile of
parcels. Ermine tut-tutted and gave Alex a
meaning look, and Alex knew what that look
meant. It meant that she should put her foot
down, scold Lucy for prying, but she was suddenly
tired of her family.

She realised, with a start of dismay, that she was
actually looking forward to getting back home—
and that was strange as well, her thinking of the
Bayswater flat as home! Greg might be all the
things, all the bad things she thought him, but he
didn't tear her apart as Ermine and her sister did.
She loved them both but they were so different,
and it wasn't just the seventeen-year age gap that
separated them. She could get on with either of
them alone, but when they were together, sniping
at each other, she felt as though she was caught in
the crossfire.

Lucy had torn the plastic ties from the largest
box and was stripping away layers of tissue paper
before bringing the contents into the open. 'Ooh!'
she gasped as layers of green chiffon slid through
her hands. 'This is going to take some living up to!
Just remember, dear sister—this is *my* party, you'll
have enough going for you with Greg being
uxorious, isn't that a lovely word—I hope it
means what I think it does. He'll have to buy me
something as well,' her eyes sparkled. 'I'll ring him
up and tell him so, and it had better be as good as
this, because I'm not taking second place at my
own party!'

'Lucy,' Ermine interfered although Alex had
been silently praying that she wouldn't, 'you
couldn't take anything from that man!'

'Why ever not?' Lucy made her blue eyes very big and round. 'He's going to give me away, and that makes him almost my father. By the way, Alex, you forgot to ask him about that, I had to do it myself, but it's all right, he said he would.'

Her aunt, who had been sitting open-mouthed with the teapot in her hand, suddenly came to life, slamming the teapot down on the table. 'This is too much!' She was angry and her eyes glittered. 'After the way he treated Alex! Lucy, I'm ashamed of you!'

Alex thought she ought to pour some oil on the waters before they became too troubled, before Lucy said something unforgivable, but no soothing phrases came to mind. She was too late anyway.

'I don't blame him,' Lucy spat the words at her aunt. 'He's Alex's husband, she should have done what he wanted, gone with him. Oh yes, I know it was all my fault, but that doesn't matter. She didn't *have* to stay with me, you could have looked after me. YOU knew it was just a hangover, same as he did!'

'Disgusting!' Ermine compressed her lips further and there were green sparks in her eyes. 'That hateful man . . .' and Alex sat waiting for the explosion, and it came, as she knew it would, as it always did when Lucy and their aunt were quarrelling.

'He's not hateful at all, he's very nice, and he understands.' Lucy's temper was lost and her control had gone with it. 'I like Greg—I wouldn't marry him, he's far too old, but I like him. And he's going to make things a lot easier for me. I want a nice wedding with all the trimmings, and why shouldn't Greg pay for it? He's Alex's husband and he's rolling!' Lucy flung the green chiffon back into its box and stormed out of the room.

'Oh dear, what are we going to do with her?' Ermine was weeping copiously into her handkerchief. 'Now you know why I couldn't be left with her, Alex. She's so crude, so rude . . .'

Alex took up her usual role as peacemaker. 'Just young and a bit thoughtless. You know she always says what she thinks, but she's very honest . . .'

'No, she's not.' Ermine emerged from the handkerchief and her eyes were glittering spitefully. 'She twists everything to her own advantage, saying I knew when I only suspected. I couldn't be sure. Trying to put the blame on me—how could anybody think such a thing about me? It's true, I dislike your husband, and I was almost glad when you found out for yourself what sort of man he was, but that was only because I knew he wasn't good enough for you, that he'd make you unhappy. He's done it once and he'll do it again, you'll see,' and Ermine resumed her weeping.

Alex made soothing noises; words weren't any use, not when Ermine was working up to a small hysteria, and she disengaged her aunt's clutching fingers when Ermine started to suggest, 'Come back here, Alex, come back before you get hurt again . . .'

'I have to give it a second chance.' Alex was in a corner and she could see no way out, not without spoiling things for Lucy. 'Make a fresh pot of tea,' she suggested, 'while I go down and smooth Lucy's feathers. I'll pick up my spectacles at the same time.' And she fled from the room and down the stairs to the basement where Lucy was washing up her breakfast things with angry fervour.

'Cool down,' Alex advised her sister. 'You'll break every plate in the place.'

'Cool down!' Lucy swung round with the dripping dishmop poised as though for war. 'When that old ... Oh!' she once more erupted into wrath. 'Take my advice, Alex, and get on back to your husband, or you'll be like she is. It'll be you sitting at the window, watching the world go by.'

'Not so much of the "old"!' Alex protested. 'Ermine's only thirty-five.'

'You could have fooled me!' Lucy was simmering down, the words came out as a mutter.

'And what was the favour you wanted to ask?' Alex attempted a diversion and it worked. Lucy forgot her wrath instantly.

'Money,' she grinned apologetically. 'Can you lend me some, please? I have to pay my share of a month's rent in advance before I can move in with the girls ...'

'Fifteen pounds?' Alex ventured the sum, praying that it would be enough. 'But since Greg's paying for the wedding,' she suggested slyly, 'couldn't you draw on your savings?'

'Oh, that!' Lucy shrugged it off. 'I only said that to get Aunty's goat. Greg isn't paying, at least not for everything—and you're an angel, Alex. Fifteen pounds, that'll be fine, I'll pay you back after I get married!'

It was nearly seven o'clock before Alex finally got herself into the taxi that was to take her back to Bayswater. Ermine had taken more than the usual amount of soothing before she was nearly normal, and then Lucy had looked in on her way out to a date with her fiancé and she and Ermine had faced each other like two fighting cocks. Of course, Lucy couldn't resist making things worse by reminding Alex that it was time she was back with her husband.

'He thinks you're shopping and he'll start wondering soon, now that all the shops are closed. I shouldn't wonder if he didn't come round here to fetch you,' Lucy said maliciously, savouring every word, and Alex gathered up her parcels in a hurry, told her aunt not to worry about a thing and fled.

CHAPTER FIVE

GREG was waiting for her in the hall of the flat, his face a mask, impenetrable and hard; there was also a gleam in his eyes which caused her concern, but she'd had enough upsets for one day. She had been looking forward to coming home—at this point she caught herself up; she was to stop thinking of this as home. It wasn't, not hers. This was Greg's place, and from the look he was giving her, she was going to be incarcerated within its walls for the next six months.

She stalked past him to the bedroom without saying a word and dumped her parcels on the bed, then she took off her coat and returned to the hall where he was still standing.

'What's wrong now?' she demanded.

'You said you were going shopping.' He made it sound like an accusation and she flared up, her eyes sparkling with irritation.

'So, I *have* been shopping,' she gestured through the open door of her bedroom to the tumble of boxes and carrier bags that lay unopened on her bed. 'And then I went to Kensington to see Ermine. Is that a crime?'

'Only in so far as you didn't tell me,' he pointed out without heat. 'I've been expecting you since about six o'clock.'

'Why don't you tie me to the table leg?' Her irritation was growing and the words spilled out almost against her will. Hadn't she promised herself that she would be cool and contained; that it was no use trying to match words with Greg— and she heard her tongue busily wagging on. 'Or you could get some handcuffs and shackle me to the bedpost,' she suggested bitingly, her mouth twisting into a bitter mockery of a smile. 'I didn't know I was going to be a prisoner.'

'And I didn't know you were going to see your aunt,' he snapped back at her.

'You have a list of proscibed persons?' The irritation was dying, to be replaced by a chilly weariness. 'You must give me a copy so I know who's on the forbidden list.'

'There's no list,' he sounded equally weary. 'You can go where you like, do what you like, but I must insist that you tell me where you're going and what time you'll be back.' He waved a hand towards the kitchen. 'I've had to order dinner without knowing when you'd be here to eat it, and if you don't like what I've ordered, you'll have to go without.'

'Charming!' she glared at him stonily. 'In that case, I'd better start doing the cooking, at least I shall be able to eat what I want and it'll give me something to do while I'm tied to the table leg. Make sure the rope's long enough for me to move about.'

'Thank you, my dear.' He was being overly polite. 'I thought you'd never offer.' He took her arm and steered her towards the kitchen. 'What did Lucy want of you?'

'That's none of your business.' Alex wriggled, but her arm remained trapped.

'I've made it my business.' His fingers dug into the thin layer of flesh covering the fragile bones. 'Take a look at yourself, you're looking harassed. I've told Lucy, if she wants anything, she's to come to me. I'm not having you run off your feet dancing attendance on your family. You're going to take things easily until you stop looking like a ghost.'

'Except what I have to do for you!' she reminded him sharply. 'And if I have to work for anybody, I'd prefer to do it for a stranger. I remember very well what it was like when I worked for you before, it was sheer hell at times. I often wondered how I stuck it.'

They were in the kitchen and Greg still retained his hold on her arm. 'It won't be so bad this time,' he said unsympathetically. 'You know the standards I expect, and in any case, I've decided not to start yet, not until you're looking better.'

'And are you going to pay me the usual rates?'

'Pay you? Alexandra, you're becoming mercenary!' The hardness went from his face and he chuckled. 'You'll have your bed and board, I'll clothe you and give you an allowance; in fact, it will be just as we planned three years ago.'

'With one small difference,' she pointed out glacially.

The hand left her arm and slid round her shoulders and he pulled her back to rest against him. She went unresistingly; to have struggled would have been undignified as well as useless, he was far too strong for her. 'The difference!' He was whispering it into her ear, his breath making the short hairs on her neck move slightly so that she shivered. 'Give it a little time, dear heart, and you'll find there won't be any difference at all!' His hand found her breast, caressing until she shuddered with the knowledge that despite herself, she was responding to the touch of his fingers like the strings of a harp to an experienced player. 'Mmm,' he murmured while his fingers probed pointed fullness. 'See what I mean?'

Alex shrugged herself away from him. 'I won't!'

'But the question isn't whether you will or you won't.' He still stood behind her, although now he wasn't touching her. 'It's *when* will you, and I estimate very shortly; in fact within five minutes, if I put my mind to it.'

Alex stood very still, her eyes fixed on the things on the counter as she summoned up some courage with which to defeat her deplorable weakness. She hated him, she despised him, but she still couldn't prevent her body responding to him. The courage came and she turned to face him. 'Oh dear! Are we going into the seduction routine? Please excuse me while I go and change into my chastity belt. While I'm doing that, you can bring on the dancing girls, no seduction scene is complete without them. And by the way,' she eyed him darkly, 'since I'm going to be doing the cooking, what sort of dressing do you prefer with your filet mignon, ground glass or arsenic? Oh!' She was suddenly struck by the stupidity of the situation. 'Greg, we can't go on like this, and you're a fool if you think we can. You can't expect to take up where we left off three years ago. I've changed. I'm not in love with you any more.' It was a lie, but she looked in his eyes.

'I can make you want me.' Alex couldn't be

sure, but she thought she detected an obstinate note in his voice.

'Maybe,' she answered. 'I'm human, the same as any other woman—you should know that, you've had enough of them—but I don't think you can make me say "Please", and that's the magic word, isn't it?'

Greg led her to the other end of the counter where the metal containers were stacked in the oven. 'What a pity I married a woman with a good memory. I shall have to watch what I say more carefully. Meanwhile, go and change for dinner. Put on your chastity belt if you wish, or you can doll yourself up in a full suit of armour. It won't do you any good at all.'

Somehow, the atmosphere between them had lightened, become less prickly, and Alex lost some of her tenseness. She smiled widely at him. 'A proper little Casanova, aren't you?' and she sped away to the bedroom.

From the clatter in the kitchen, she judged she hadn't time for a shower, so she scrambled herself out of the new green suit she was wearing, washed her hands and face and quickly donned a dark red caftan in a fine woollen material. She thought it looked very becoming and although it was part of the load of clothes which Greg had paid for on Monday, it wasn't one that made her feel guilty. It hadn't been all that expensive and she would get a lot of wear out of it.

'Mmm.' He surveyed her with appreciation when she returned, her face nicely made up and with the fragrance of her new bottle of perfume drifting about her. 'Chastity belt in place? Padlock secure?'

'Yes.' She seated herself at the table and some long-buried humour woke in her so that her eyes twinkled more with fun than with malice. 'And as an extra precaution, I've swallowed the key!'

On the day of Lucy's engagement party, Alex spent nearly the whole morning in the hairdresser's, where her hair was cut and shampooed and dressed in a swinging, almost shoulder-length style with the ends neatly curled under so that it looked like a bell. The time she had spent was worth it, she decided as she looked at herself in the mirror while she completed her dressing for the party. Her pale blonde tresses now shone with a silvery gleam which nicely matched the embroidery and the tiny silver beads which edged the neckline of her green chiffon.

The cost of the operation had been a bitter pill to swallow; even if she hadn't given Lucy most of her ready money, she couldn't have paid for it herself, so she used Greg's credit card and dismissed the nasty taste in her mouth by remembering that this was Lucy's party and she had to look her best for it—Greg had insisted on it! Moreover, Robert's mother had changed her mind about using her own house as a venue and had opted for a hired ballroom instead. Lucy had been on the phone about it, chortling with glee.

'Guess what, Alex? Ma-in-law-to-be has decided to hire a ballroom, isn't that a much better idea?'

'And I bet I know where she had the idea,' Alex said sarcastically.

'I didn't say a word,' Lucy protested with

innocence. 'All I said was that if she was going to
hold it in her house, she'd better roll up her prized
Oriental carpets and stow away anything break-
able. Aren't I clever?'

'Too clever for your own good, sometimes,'
Alex had snorted, but it wasn't really a reprimand.
She was beginning to admire Lucy's self-centred
machinations and her abounding self-confidence.
Her admiration was slightly tinged with envy, her
own confidence in herself had taken a few knocks
lately.

It was now—she counted up on her fingers—
two weeks and six days since she had gone back to
live with her husband and two weeks and three
days since she had decided it was a situation she
could handle. She had been woefully wrong, of
course! Even filling her mind with his disgusting
behaviour hadn't helped very much. Greg smiled
at her and she found herself smiling back, he said
something witty or sarcastic and she had to
smother her chuckle. He put a hand on her
shoulder and her surface layer of ice started to
melt, so that when he removed the hand, she felt
cold and lonely. It was very strange that she could
have been so bitter for the years while he was not
there and then start forgetting bitterness as soon as
he put in an appearance again.

Now, when she thought about it, his walking
out seemed more of a dream than anything else,
the cutting edges of that memory didn't seem as
sharp or painful any longer, and she had to go
away into another room, live it all over again, in
order to bring back the feeling of disgust and the
sense of ill-usage. She supposed it was one of the

penalties of being in love with a man; reason and common sense flew out of the window and even humiliation lost its sting. He could still stir her and situated as she was, in daily contact with him, her chilly aloofness took a great deal of maintaining.

'Very nice.' Greg came quietly behind her as she sat at the dressing table, putting the final touches to her face. Alex scowled at him in the mirror and set her lipstick down. Her hand was shaking too much to guarantee a clear outline.

'I prefer to be alone to do this,' she said icily, studiously avoiding looking directly at him, even in the mirror. He looked quite distinguished, and involuntarily her eyes flicked over him while she pretended to hunt for another lipstick. No, she decided, she couldn't be blamed for feeling as she did; Greg had it all! His black jacket fitted smoothly across his shoulders, the white shirt made his face look darker than ever and his well tailored black trousers clung to his lean hips before going on for ever down his long legs. 'God's gift to the female sex!' She tried to whip herself up into a disgusted frame of mind while all the time remembering how smooth his skin was under the shirt, how her fingers had once slid silkily over it.

'Do you want something?' she muttered.

'My wife.' He was sparing of words and left her in no doubt as to his meaning.

She coloured and shook her head as she fumbled with the stopper of a perfume bottle. 'No, Greg, I'm here under duress and I don't want you. Go away and let me finish dressing or we're going to be late.'

'I can't tempt you?' His hands were on her shoulders and she shivered at his touch, leaning away from him, closer to the mirror to smooth away a smear of face powder. 'You're shivering,' he jeered. 'What with, anticipation?'

'No, distaste.' She slid from underneath his hands, going swiftly to the bed where her dress was spread ready. Greg raised a mocking eyebrow and shrugged.

'So you tell lies as well.' He sounded amused, like some superior being watching the useless struggles of a captive. 'Go ahead, Alexandra, tell yourself all the lies you please, it won't help you and it won't make them true. Nobody's perfect, not me, not Lucy, not your dear little aunt and certainly not you. One day you'll open those blind eyes of yours and see people as they really are and not as you think they should be. I'll wait, but I'm not spending any more time in waiting than I can avoid. If you won't see for yourself, I'll damn well force you to see!' He turned from her and strode back into his own room, pausing at the door to look back at her with jeering amusement. 'You really should keep this door locked, darling. That's why I left the key on your side.'

Alex struggled into her dress and ran after him to slam the door and turn the key viciously. After which she leaned back against the door panels, her bosom rising and falling rapidly with her shortened breath. Fear? Excitement? She couldn't put a name to the emotion that possessed her but it definitely had a therapeutic value; it caused the adrenalin in her blood to increase by about a hundred per cent, brought a stain of colour to her normally pale cheeks and made her eyes look brighter.

By the time she had finished dressing and went to meet him in the lounge, her adrenalin supply was back to normal and she was her usual calm, composed self. While she had waited for her cheeks to cool and her heartbeat to steady down, she had chewed over what he had said. Of course she knew nobody was perfect, she made no claims to be that herself, but her imperfections were minor compared with her husband's. Nobody could call her a libertine or whatever the female equivalent was.

Part of what he had said was true, though—she was only just finding out about Lucy. It was strange how people grew up and you didn't notice. Under all that froth on the surface, Lucy was firm, level-headed and utterly adult, more adult than Alex was herself. Thinking of her sister brought Alex back to the matter in hand, which was getting to the party on time, and she hurried out into the lounge where Greg was waiting for her, seated on the chesterfield and with the smoke from a cigarette drifting in pale blue whorls about his head.

'I'm ready,' she informed him briskly, then flushed as his eyes slid over her from head to toe, taking in the drift of green chiffon and her narrow, silver-strapped sandals.

'You pay for dressing,' he observed. 'What about a coat?'

'My tweed,' she was sturdy about it. 'It's what I always wear.'

'Not good enough,' he stilled her protest with a

wave of his hand. 'Robert's mother is expecting something much grander than that from my wife.' His eyes glittered with puckish humour. 'She'll think I'm forcing you to economise.' He gestured at a large box beside him. 'I realised you hadn't bothered, so I bothered for you. Wear that.'

Alex lifted the lid and looked down at the mink before she sighed regretfully and replaced the tissue wrappings. 'No, thank you.'

'Wear it, my love, I didn't ask if you wanted to.'

'An order?' She became haughty.

'Precisely—and another thing, your engagement ring, you remember it? You left it with me to have it made smaller. Here it is, although it will still be too big, I suppose.'

She stood, straight and still, looking down at him where he lounged. 'I'm not some charity brat,' she snapped vehemently. 'I will not be condescended to!'

'Maybe not, but you must consider my image.' A smile lurked at the corner of his mouth. 'Robert Latchford's mother knows my bank balance to the nearest fraction of a penny, I daresay, she's that type of woman. So look on this as window dressing if you like. We are going to create a good impression for your sister's sake.'

'And you don't think we can do that without my being dressed up like some favourite in a sultan's harem?' Alex snorted in disgust.

'Your ring, my love.' Greg paid no heed to her protest. 'You wore it before without any feeling of condescension. Put it and the coat on and we'll go. Don't you realise how much time you've wasted, you'll make us late!'

She allowed him to force the ring over her knuckle and looked down balefully at the square emerald. 'Ostentation!' she snapped tartly. 'And the coat; a jacket or a shoulder cape would have been quite sufficient, if your mind was on window dressing and the impression we'd make. There was no need for this vulgar parade of wealth.'

'I was thinking about next winter,' Greg murmured. 'I wouldn't like to think of you freezing.'

Alex waited until she was seated in the car before she replied to that one. 'I shan't be here next winter—and,' she added cattily, 'since you insist, I shall wear this coat. I'll wear it and wear it until it's in tatters, and you'll lose a lot of money on it and serve you right!'

His hand left the wheel and came to rest on her knee. 'Oh, I think you'll be here next winter, my dear.'

'Is that a threat?' She raised her eyebrows and in the faint light from the dashboard, she thought she saw the ghost of an amused smile curl his lips and soften the harsh planes of his face.

'No, not a threat,' he gave an almost silent chuckle. 'More of a promise, I'd say.'

Alex reached out a hand and picked up his fingers from where they rested warmly on her knee, examined them briefly with an expression of disdain, gave a definite sniff and ostentatiously dropped them back on the steering wheel.

'Getting nervous?' His amusement increased and there was an overt insinuation in his voice.

'I've a right to be, haven't I?' Deliberately, she misunderstood him. 'This is the first time I shall be meeting Robert's mother. She's asked us to tea, Ermine and me, on several occasions, but of course we couldn't go. Afternoon visiting's for the idle rich, not for poor working girls. The little notes were always addressed to Miss Alexandra and Miss Ermine Winter, and although I suppose Lucy's made a stab at explaining—I wonder if she's put it down to Women's Lib—there are bound to be one or two awkward moments tonight. Ah well,' she sighed with a martyred air and sat well back in her seat, 'as I said before, I shall leave it all to you, you're the expert. I don't see why I should perjure myself thinking up excuses for your bad behaviour, not when I'm the injured and blameless party.'

'But I told you, I never explain.'

'This time you'll have to,' she told him grumpily. 'It's all right for you, you don't care what people think, but I'm not standing round in a pool of embarrassment trying to think up an excuse for producing a husband after three years. If Robert's mother was just a casual acquaintance, I wouldn't mind so much, but she's going to be Lucy's mother-in-law and I don't want her looking down her nose at my sister. She's done enough of that already, according to Lucy.'

Greg's long fingers came back to her knee and when she tried to remove them, he squeezed on the sensitive nerve. 'Don't brawl in the car, darling, it disturbs my concentration. I've told you before, there won't be any questions. You'll be greeted with enthusiasm or perhaps fawning admiration and any periods in your life that don't stand examination will be skilfully avoided.' Alex let his hand rest where it was and was shocked and surprised to discover how warm and comforting it was.

'Alex, you look gorgeous!' Lucy came speeding into the ladies' cloakroom where Alex was repairing the slight damage which had occurred to her hair and face during the ride. 'Come on,' Lucy was in a fever of impatience, 'you look quite all right and Ma-in-law-to-be is awaiting your arrival with bated breath. Did you know——' She gave a giggle of pure mirth and allowed her voice to drop an octave or so as she mimicked a stately utterance:

'Of course, the Malluses have been family friends for twenty-five years and I have followed dear Gregory's wonderful career with the greatest interest.'

She grasped Alex's hand and towed her out into the ballroom. 'Isn't it lovely?' she demanded, 'and so much better than trying to crowd everybody into a house. I'll say that for Robert's mother, when she does something, she does it properly. The band's good as well, and the buffet looks super. What do you think of my dress?' Lucy twirled, sending cream-coloured silk swirling about her ankles. 'This is the ingénue approach—do you think it suits me? And wasn't it good of Greg to pay for it? If I'd have had to buy something for myself, it wouldn't have been half as nice.'

The years of quiet living had made Alex unused to large parties, she hardly knew what to do with herself and was grateful for Greg's presence at her side. He stayed there all the time except for one dance which he allowed her with Robert; apart from that, he claimed all the others. Robert's mother was the essence of hospitality and gratification, so that it was hard to remember that there had been a time when she had disapproved of Lucy—but, Alex congratulated herself, maybe that had nothing to do with Greg! Lucy herself had worked hard for Mrs Latchford's approbation and at a guess, the dress Lucy was wearing had been chosen with Robert's mother in mind. It was discreet, demure and utterly lacking in impact; in it Lucy looked a sweet seventeen-year-old in whose mouth butter wouldn't melt. Alex smiled to herself grimly. Mrs Latchford was due for a few surprises! Lucy of the forthright tongue and tearing temper would emerge eventually, but not before the wedding.

'Enjoyed yourself?' Greg was helping her off with her coat in the peace of their flat, and Alex kicked off her strappy sandals with a moan of relief and pattered kitchenwards in her stockinged feet, holding the hem of her dress well clear of the floor.

'So-so,' she admitted as she filled the kettle. 'I don't think I'm the convivial type, though, it did get very noisy after a while.'

'No, you're more the "small, select dinner party" woman. We shall have to give a few of those, you'll do them beautifully.' He slanted a mocking glance down at her. 'There weren't any awkward questions, though. You see, it was just as I said, nobody dared ask.'

'They didn't ask.' Alex reached for the teapot, warmed it and measured in the tea. 'They just looked. I could see their brains whizzing round, doing acrobatics, trying to work it out for themselves.'

He was standing too close to her, she could feel the warmth of his body creeping through the thin chiffon and touching her skin. For a moment she wished with all her heart that she had just one speck of Lucy's forthrightness. Lucy would have turned round to him and said, 'Go away, darling, you're turning me on,' but Alex couldn't do that. Instead, she moved away from him slightly and reached for the cups and saucers.

'Do you want anything to eat? Some soup or a sandwich?' Her voice squeaked a bit and increased her embarrassment.

'You know what I want.' Greg had moved in on her again and his hands were on her shoulders, turning her to face him. He made no attempt to disguise his desire and she became fascinated by the sensuous curve of his mouth. Dully, she heard the kettle switch itself off and made no attempt to even put out a hand to it.

'No!' It came as a desperate whisper and she backed against the counter trying hard to remember, but the memories were blurred and she found herself making excuses for him. 'No,' she repeated as his finger slid from her cheek to her throat and then began an insidious downward glide. Tears of humiliation started in her eyes; he could do this to her with only one finger! 'Please!' It was a muttered entreaty through shaking lips.

The finger stopped its progress and his arms went round her, pulling her close to him so that through the thin stuff of her dress she could feel the hard strength of his body. 'The word I've been waiting for.' His voice was husky and she could only watch his mouth as it came closer, hypnotised by the curve of it.

'I didn't mean it like that,' she moaned as he began an assault on her senses, pushing the chiffon aside to reach the silken smoothness beneath it.

'Too late,' he nuzzled behind her ear, and then the old magic was back, the magic she had tried so hard to kill, and she was tumbling into his arms just as she'd tumbled three years ago, so that the three years was as nothing, as if they had never been, and there was nothing to keep them apart; no suspicion, no distrust, and she wasn't despising or hating him any longer.

Her mind flipped back in time to an occasion very much like this, only she had been much more discreetly dressed then—a suit, she remembered, not an evening dress, and Greg had dragged her to the door and pushed her outside on to the mat. 'Go home,' he had told her sternly. 'We'll continue this tomorrow, it'll be safer for you that way.' And she had almost danced all the way back to Kensington, her head in the clouds and the stars nearly touching her shoulders.

But this was different—or, her drugged mind refused to work properly, was it so different? She felt just the same now as she'd felt then, weak and very willing. Greg might be despicable, but she still loved him. Tomorrow maybe, she would despise herself, but tomorrow was a whole night away. Her arms went round his shoulders and she softened against him, a sweet gladness filling her as she felt his body leap to meet hers.

'Much too late,' his voice in her ear was thick and hoarse, 'and the kitchen's no place for what I have in mind.' And Alex lay against him, her eyes and her mind closed to everything but the present. Yesterday and tomorrow, they didn't matter, nothing mattered but that it had been so long and she wanted and needed him so desperately.

The only thing that remembered him was her body, and that was a traitor to her mind. It didn't care about his women or his bad behaviour, it was clamouring for him, demanding with an insistence she could no longer deny.

CHAPTER SIX

THE shrill note of the telephone on Greg's side of the bed woke her and she opened her eyes to bright spring sunlight. Muzzily, she stretched out an arm and waved it about in an effort to locate the instrument, and then, when the bell stopped ringing, she heard his voice giving the number.

'Mmm,' he said. 'Just a moment, I'll see if she's awake,' and then, with no attempt to disguise her nearness to him, not even a perfunctory hand over the mouthpiece, he leaned over her. 'Darling, wake up. It's your aunt, and she wants to speak to you.'

Alex grabbed the handset from him and glared at him over the edge of it as she lifted it to her ear. He was laughing at her—he had no shame!

'Hullo, Ermine, is anything wrong?' In her effort to sound just the same as usual, she heard herself being stilted.

'Alex! Oh dear, thank heaven you're at home! I was worried you might be out or that you'd still be asleep, and I didn't want to wake you up.'

'Wake me up?' Alex stifled a yawn and looked around for a clock. 'What time is it?'

'After ten.' Ermine was apologetic in a breathy fashion. 'I'm sorry if I've disturbed you, I remembered about the party, but I felt sure you'd be up and about before this, although you could have slept late, I suppose. You're not like Lucy, so used to a mad whirl and going to bed just when it's breaking dawn.'

'You didn't come,' Alex accused.

Ermine was gently indignant. 'But you couldn't expect me to, dear. All the way across London and in the dark . . .' She went on with her protest, but Alex was only listening with half an ear. Her mind was back at the party, to her dance with Robert, and she could hear his stiffly rueful tones, 'I offered to both bring and take your aunt home, Alex, but she refused', and then there had been Lucy's angry growl in the privacy of the ladies' room. 'Aunty's being a pest, as usual. She knows how short I am of family and Robert has simply hundreds of relatives and they've all come—you'd have thought, just this once, she'd have made an effort, wouldn't you? But no—we offered a taxi door to door, both ways, and when she wouldn't hear of that, Robert said he'd fetch her himself and take her home afterwards and the answer was still "No". I even offered to ring you and get you and Greg to pick her up, but she went right off the deep end! Nothing would get her within seeing distance of the Monster—that's what she calls Greg.'

'You were offered transport,' Alex broke in on Ermine's garbled speech, troubled at finding herself slightly out of patience. She'd never felt like this before.

'I know, dear, but . . .' Ermine launched immediately into another pathetic set of excuses and Alex breathed deeply while she made soothing noises down the phone. She supposed she should be kinder, her aunt was possibly lonely and wishful to talk to a sympathetic audience. Apart from office hours, Ermine led a lonely life, never exchanging more than a polite 'good day' with anybody.

'Where are you phoning from?' Alex broke in at last. 'Is anything wrong?'

'From the basement. I've had to come down here.'

Alex snapped bolt upright in bed and fumbled for the sheet to pull over herself. At ten o'clock in the morning, Ermine should be comfortably established in her office and surrounded by income tax supplicants. 'Why aren't you at work?' she demanded. 'Are you ill—have you fallen?'

'I can't explain,' came the whimper over the wire. 'Not over the phone. Please, Alex, there's nobody else I can talk to.' And the connection was broken as Ermine let her end of the phone drop into its cradle.

Greg came back into the room, swathed in a very short towelling robe which came to an end well above his knees, his hair was damp and he was freshly shaved so that he smelled nicely of a masculine eau de cologne. 'Tea or coffee?' he enquired, but Alex hardly heard him. She was too busy hunting around for an accessible piece of cloth to cover her nakedness. Finally she dragged the bedspread about her, winding it round herself and struggling to keep the fringed ends in position.

'Anything,' she said absently. 'Just a hot drink. No!' as he came towards her, chuckling at the way the bedspread was behaving, 'leave me alone, I'm going for a shower.'

'But is this display of modesty really necessary?' Greg was still amused and a charming smile curved his lips. 'Alexandra! You've been all night with me without a stitch between us . . .'

'Forget it!' Worry made her voice sharp as she interrupted.

The smile was instantly transformed into a heavy scowl. 'No, I won't bloody well forget it!' he snarled the words as he seized a handful of bedspread, effectively stopping her progress towards the door. 'What in hell are you playing at? I thought we had it all ironed out . . .'

'. . . I'm not playing at anything!' She struggled to twist free of the encompassing folds. 'Last night was last night; I'm not ashamed of it, but this morning's different. Last night I wanted you . . .'

'. . . And this morning, you don't!' His eyebrows were no longer set in the usual Mephisthophelean arch, they were a solid black bar of scowl above his eyes. Alex saw the warning flare in those eyes, but she ignored it, her mind was on getting showered, dressed and over to Ermine, until with furious hands he stripped away the folds of material, prising apart her clutching fingers ruthlessly. 'Come back to bed, my dear, and I'll demonstrate your error.'

'No, Greg,' she struggled against him. 'You don't understand, Ermine needs me . . .' but her protests were useless. He picked her up and practically threw her on to the bed with sufficient force so that she bounced on the well sprung mattress, and when she attempted to skid off the other side, he let his whole weight drop on her, holding her fast.

'Oh, but I do understand, it's you who's not understanding,' he ground the words out savagely.

'Last night wasn't just last night, not for me. For me, it's tomorrow night, tonight and all the other nights when I want you and you want me. And it would be this morning as well, if I want; which I did—but I don't now!' He lifted himself away from her. 'Go and shower,' and as she made another grab at the bedspread, 'no, go as you are, my modest little wife. Streak! I'll be watching.'

Showered and wrapped in a bath towel, Alex made her way back to her own bedroom on bare feet, to find Greg already dressed in fawn cords and a tobacco brown pullover over a cream silk shirt. He was sitting on the bed with her purse open in his hand.

'Dress,' he said curtly, and tossed the purse to her. Awkwardly, she caught it, opened it and surveyed the empty interior with dismay before erupting into fury.

'Where's my money? There was over five pounds in that purse, what have you done with it?'

'It's here.' He reached into his hip pocket and extracted a small sheaf of notes and other things. 'Together with your cheque book and,' he waved a piece of plastic under her nose, 'Your cheque card.' He smiled, but there was no warmth in it, just a wolfish unpleasantness. 'They're no use to you or anybody else now. I've just phoned your bank, on your behalf, to tell them you've discovered you've lost both. The bank is stopping payment at once so, even if you manage to get them back, which you won't, it won't do you a bit of good. You've a few things to learn, my girl, and the first lesson is that you don't treat me as a one-night stand to satisfy your needs.'

'I did not!' she protested vehemently.

'Yes, you did!' He was as angry as she. 'You used me, Alexandra, you admitted it. Now get dressed and come to breakfast, and after that, I'll drive you to Kensington.'

'Then get out of my room while I dress!' she hissed.

'No.' He settled back on the bed, the anger fading from his face to be replaced by a look of sardonic amusement. 'I'll stay here and watch—in fact, I'll help. My, my!' as she grabbed a load of underwear from a drawer. 'Frillies! So that's what you wear under that prissy exterior.' He made a long arm and seized on something lace-trimmed and filmy, arching his eyebrows devilishly as he swung the garment from his fingers. 'These things are a dead giveaway, darling; it's no wonder you're so good in bed.'

Alex grew calm and cold, but only after she had torn the garment from his hands. She looked at his length sprawled easily on her bed and tilted her chin. 'If you must lie on my bed,' she observed icily, 'please take your shoes off.' And then she collected what further clothes she required and returned to the bathroom, where she hurriedly dressed herself.

When she emerged, neat in a pair of brown slacks, a pink silk shirt and a tan suede sleeveless jacket, it was to sniff at the aroma of coffee coming from the kitchen together with the stronger smell of burning toast. Greg was at it again! Give him a bit of mosaic pavement and he could reconstruct it in its entirety, show him the bare outlines of a Roman fort and he would unerringly fill in the bathhouse, the commandant's dwelling, the barracks, the granary and the cookhouse, but he only had to look at a gas jet or an electrical appliance to foul it up! This time, by the smell, he'd managed to reduce the toaster to a smoking ruin.

Swiftly, Alex fled back to the bedroom, stuffed her feet into a pair of soft casuals, brushed her hair into a swinging silver bell and flicked a powder puff over her face. Lipstick could wait until after breakfast, she always ate it off at mealtimes.

She went down the hallway and paused in the doorway to the kitchen, peering at him through the smoke-filled atmosphere with a look compounded of hate and exasperation.

'Can't you do anything right?' she demanded shrilly. 'Switch it off!'

Greg raised his head from a rapt contemplation of the toaster where columns of smoke were rising from the flames flickering in the slots. 'It's supposed to switch itself off,' he said indignantly, and Alex reached across him to pull out the plug from the socket just as he began to prod the smouldering mass with the point of the carving knife. She found her lips twitching with reluctant amusement and swiftly stopped herself softening towards him.

'I know the Romans didn't have electricity, but shouldn't you read up a little about it?' she snapped it at him, and then, 'Oh, go and open a window before we choke to death! What on earth have you got in here, anyway?' She tipped up the toaster and exhumed two sausage-like, smouldering corpses.

Greg flung open the window and turned back to her. 'I couldn't find any bread, only rolls, so I pushed a couple of those in. The coffee's all right, though.' He peered over her shoulder at the toaster. 'Will it go again, or should we have a new one?'

Alex pushed him out of the way as she went to the breadbin, took out another four rolls, split them and put them on the wire tray under the grill of the electric cooker and to save further accidents, stood and watched them while they browned. 'We'll try it when it's been cleaned out—meanwhile,' she shovelled the toasted rolls on to a plate and dumped it on the table, 'could we hurry, please? Ermine sounded rather urgent and she hasn't the slightest idea of how long it will take me to get across London.'

'Ah yes, your aunt,' Greg scowled, and the little lightening of the atmosphere caused by the contretemps with the toaster vanished as though it had never been. 'I'll drive you there, come in with you and drive you back when you've sorted out the problem.'

Alex gulped the remainder of her coffee, stood up and looked at him nastily. 'You can drive me there and drive me back, but you don't come into the house. Ermine's in a state and you're the last person she'll want to see, you'll have to wait outside. She calls you the Monster and I'm beginning to agree with her—I've quite a few bruises to prove it. In fact,' she straightened her back and the green flecks sparked in her eyes, 'if she's very upset, I shan't leave her. You can come back here on your own.'

'No.' Greg looked at her, holding her gaze with his own until her eyes fell before his. 'You'll come back with me, my dear wife, or word will get around that you've walked out on me for the second time. Mrs Latchford will immediately suspect your whole family is prone to frivolous inconstancy and Lucy's engagement won't last five minutes.'

'You wouldn't!' She took a step back from him, aghast. 'You told Lucy it would be all right, you paid for her dress—she trusts you!'

'Try me,' he advised as he buttered a toasted roll with precision, then he raised his coffee cup to her in a mock salute. 'To us, my dear, until the passion dies!'

At the Kensington house, Alex rummaged in her bag and found the key to the door of the basement flat, then she gasped with outrage as Greg deftly removed it from her fingers and led the way down the area steps.

'I said you weren't to come in,' she scolded. 'I told you . . .'

'You tell me nothing!' He turned, halfway down the steps, his fingers holding the handrail, to look back up at her. His face was a hard mask and his eyes were dark and unfathomable, while behind them, anger and distaste were lurking.

Alex folded her lips tightly against the hot words on her tongue and swished by him as he unlocked and opened the door. She would have liked to slam it in his face, trapping his fingers in it, maybe even breaking a couple of them, and she wondered if he would follow her. She needn't have bothered wondering, because as she walked through the door of the kitchen-cum-lounge overlooking the garden, he was right behind her and before she could say a word to Ermine, who was huddled in a chair, Greg had passed her to stand in front of her aunt.

'I've brought my wife,' he looked coldly down at Ermine's pale face. 'I'm now going back to sit in the car. If Alexandra doesn't join me there in twenty minutes' time, I shall come back and fetch her.'

Ermine looked up at him and idly Alex noted that there was a fugitive triumph in her aunt's eyes, as though in some way Greg had been humbled. 'And if Alex doesn't want to go with you?' Ermine's eyes glittered, so much greener than her own. 'If she decides that she prefers to stay here with me?'

'Alexandra knows what she has to do.' Greg's face and voice became colder.

'She may prefer to be guided by me.' Ermine smiled a tight, mirthless smile.

'Not this time.' He reached an arm, slipped it round his wife's waist and drew her to his side. 'She knows the consequences of doing something as stupid as that.' Alex began to feel like a bone that two dogs were fighting over, so she interrupted brightly,

'Half an hour, or was it twenty minutes, Greg? Then you'd better go out to the car and wait, starting from now!' And she looked pointedly at the kitchen clock before turning back to see him fling out of the room with a pronounced slam of the door. The slam of the outer door was even more violent, it rattled the window in what had been Lucy's room.

'Alex!' All Ermine's softness and hesitation were gone. 'Alex!' Her voice became sharp as she demanded her niece's attention. 'When I rang this morning, Greg answered the phone. He said he'd wake you and I heard him call you, he didn't put the phone down. Are you sleeping with him?'

'Yes!' Alex said bluntly, making no attempt at an easy answer, she was irritated at what she could only call an unwarranted invasion of her privacy.

'He—he forced you?' Ermine opened wide, horrified eyes.

'No, certainly not.' Alex put her head thoughtfully on one side. 'Greg wouldn't force himself on any woman. I was quite willing—we *are* married, you know, and I believe it's not unusual for married couples to sleep together. In any case, it's nothing new to us, we've done it before. And now,' she made a desperate attempt to change the subject, 'what is it you wanted me for? Are you ill? You don't look very well.'

'How can I be well?' Ermine was almost crying and she refused to be diverted from her chosen topic. 'I'm worried about you all the time. My dear, why on earth did you go back to that man, and now how on earth are you going to get a divorce? Have you thought?' Her face whitened and her eyes became too big for it. 'He could make you pregnant. What would we do if that happened? You'd never be free of him.'

'Stop it!' Alex stamped her foot for emphasis. 'Ermine, will you listen! I told you—Greg and I are having a second try at making this marriage work. Six months, I told you that, so stop going into wild fantasies. More important, you tell me why you called this morning, why you had me come over here and why you're here in the basement flat. What's wrong with your own place, have you got a burst or something?'

'I can't live there any longer,' Ermine declared mulishly. 'Not on the ground floor, with people forever coming and going in and out. It could be anybody, you know; half the time the tenants don't lock the door, they leave it on the latch so I never know who's come in. It could be a burglar or a housebreaker. I'm going to move down here.'

'But you can't!' Alex seethed with exasperation. 'You know this flat's to let, it's been advertised. Mr Dobey, the solicitor, might find a tenant at any moment.'

'Then the new tenant can have that pathetic little place you crammed me into.' Ermine's eyes glittered spitefully, and Alex sighed.

'It won't do, Ermine. This is the flat for letting, and in any case, with it being larger, the rent's higher and I need the money for the mortgage repayments. What's made you suddenly dissatisfied? You chose your own place, nobody forced you to take the flat on the ground floor.'

Ermine ignored the question of choice and harked back to the money problem. 'Mortgage repayments,' she sneered. 'Why should you have to pay all that interest?'

'But you said you didn't want to live down here, that it was claustrophobic—like being buried alive . . .'

'I've changed my mind, as I have every right to do,' Ermine said superciliously. 'I feel safer down here and I've taken a few days off to move my things.'

'And you've dragged me all the way over here just for that!' Swiftly rising temper made Alex's voice grow a cutting edge, she heard it and brought herself under control, but Ermine hadn't noticed. She continued as though Alex hadn't uttered.

'I'm only asking one small favour from you, Alex. It isn't much, you couldn't call me a demanding woman. But it upsets me when you start talking about money, rents and mortgage repayments, and I get so angry when I think of us paying all that money when we really need it ourselves.'

Alex grabbed at her self-control again and swallowed irritation, choking it back to be calm. For something to do, she went to the counter and switched on the kettle, disciplining herself to reach for cups while she fought for control. It was no good losing her temper with Ermine, that only led to floods of tears.

'It's a very good mortgage,' she observed mildly. 'The interest rate is very low and Mr Dobey said it was much better than he'd hoped for. But however low it is, somebody's invested a lot of money in this property and they're entitled to a return on their investment.'

'And you're willing to stint us so that *he* can go about buying all the women he wants?' Ermine's head jerked savagely in the direction of the street. 'Yes,' her voice rose on a note of triumph. 'Him!

You didn't know that, did you? You've been working, scrimping and saving so that he can travel round the world in luxury, while I have to do my own cooking and cleaning and exist in three pokey rooms. You don't remember, but I do, when the house was all ours and we lived properly . . .'

Ermine continued scolding and Alex went on making tea, hardly hearing a word. Only one thing had sunk in; Ermine thought Greg had put up the money for the mortgage. She waited for a lull in her aunt's list of complaints. 'You're wrong, dear,' she said quietly.

'No, I'm not!' Ermine snapped at her. 'That day when Mr Dobey came with the papers for you to sign—remember it, Alex? You sat there with him, signing our house away without even asking me if it was what I wanted. Opening the door to any Tom, Dick or Harry who could afford the rent, and you didn't care whether they were nice people or not. I made the tea for his clerk, such a nice young man; he thought we knew all about it and I didn't disabuse him. That man put up the money, *he*'s responsible. If it hadn't been for him, we shouldn't be living like this. We managed very well before, when we only let out the top floor . . .'

'Even so,' Alex remained mild, 'Greg's not making much profit from his investment. He'd get a higher rate of interest almost anywhere else, so really he's losing money. In any case, I think you're wrong, you misunderstood something. Have a cup of tea and forget about it. I'll see Mr Dobey tomorrow and ask him about you having this basement flat. I don't think he'll agree, though.'

'See the solicitor?' Ermine raised her head like a cobra striking. 'Why do you need to do that? Tell him! Tell him I'm having this flat!'

'If you're right, it would mean asking favours of Greg for your benefit.' Alex shook her head. 'I'm sure you wouldn't want me to do that, it would put you under an obligation to him, and you wouldn't like that a bit, you know you wouldn't.' While she was speaking, her mind was clicking round, considering what to do and say for the best. Her aunt was busily working herself into a fine old state which would end in hysterical tears. She realised that she'd found another resemblance between Lucy and Ermine; they both had the same mulish obstinacy and the same determination to get their own way, but this was a side issue, something she could think about later on.

For the present, it was necessary to calm Ermine down, to bring her back from the edge of angry hysteria. The thing to do was to let her talk it out; she would be better when she'd got it all off her chest, so Alex sat, sipping her tea and listening with only half an ear while she sorted the wheat from the chaff. Ermine's complaint about being on the ground floor and being disturbed and worried by the constant traffic of people in and out, that didn't hold water, it was hardly justified. Her aunt's apartment was cut off from the main hall by a soundproofed wall which had been erected especially and at enormous expense when the house had been converted.

Furthermore, the door in that wall was furnished with a rim lock, a dead lock and two bolts. Ermine was quite safe behind it and the accommodation, three large rooms and a bathroom, was more than adequate for a single person and like the other tenants, she had her own doorbell. If only Ermine would go out a bit more, meet other people and not sit around waiting for the world to come to her. Ermine at thirty-five wasn't old, although sometimes she behaved like a late Victorian. Alex slid a glance over her aunt's face as she sipped at her tea. Ermine was quite good-looking, or she could be if she stopped being so old-fashioned.

'. . . And I think *he* owes it to us!' Ermine reached a triumphant conclusion and Alex sighed again, finished her tea and collected her bag and gloves.

'I'll have to go now, dear. I mustn't keep Greg waiting too long.'

'And tell him,' her aunt was still mulishly determined, 'tell him that I should be allowed to have this flat if I want it. I've been thinking about it and it's so suitable. When this stupid six months is up and you've proved that he isn't the right man for you, you can come back here and we'll share this flat just as you and Lucy shared. I'll be here to keep you company and I'll be able to look after you . . .' She stopped speaking as Greg's footsteps came down the passage. He was almost marching and the regular beat seemed to be issuing a challenge.

Alex had the feeling that all this had happened before, and it wasn't until Greg came into the kitchen and leaned against the door frame that she realised—it *had* happened before! Three years ago, Greg had stood by a door—not this one, another door—and it hadn't been Ermine, white with determination, who was appealing to her. It had been Lucy, white, sick and moaning on a bed.

Greg had said, 'Come,' and that time she had refused. If she refused now, she might never see him again, and she didn't think she could bear to go through it all once more, not the sense of loss, the period of desperate hoping and the final despair. Some kind fate had given her a second chance, a chance to try again and not be influenced by outside things. This time she had a chance to rely on her own good sense.

Maybe later on, when for him the novelty had worn off and the gilt had disappeared from the gingerbread—when he started on the promiscuity thing—maybe then she would leave him, but it would be her own choice and she would do the walking out, which wouldn't be half as painful.

'Time's up, Alex, unless you want me to get a parking ticket.' Greg didn't smile and he made no attempt to sway her one way or the other. He was leaving it up to her. Alex took a deep breath.

'Coming now.' She turned back to her aunt. 'I'll see what I can do and ring you later in the week, but stay here for now—and stop worrying, there's a dear. 'Bye for now,' and she went out, analysing her emotions as she left the house. She could hardly believe the conclusion at which she arrived, so she started again from the beginning and worked it out once more. Yes, there was no doubt about it, she wasn't feeling guilty or particularly worried, she was feeling relieved—as though she had walked out from under a deep shadow into the sunlight.

CHAPTER SEVEN

GREG drove back to the flat in silence, but Alex was too busy with her thoughts to even notice. He garaged the car, but when she turned to enter the block of flats, his hand on her arm stopped her. It wasn't a fierce, painful grip, as so many other times it had been, but a gentle, insistent pressure that led her away in the opposite direction whether she would or not.

'We'll have lunch out today,' and he steered her along the street, turned a corner and there was the restaurant which provided the outside meals. 'We'll see what they're like at direct service.'

'You're getting tired of my cooking,' she jeered at him. 'Ah well, I knew it had to happen some time, and it has. Now that I've proved to you that I'm not suited for the task you've allotted me, perhaps you'll be sensible and give me that divorce.'

'Certainly not.' Greg studied her face. 'You're quite a good little cook, not up to Cordon Bleu standards, but that will come with time. No, today you look a little fraught, as though it would be difficult for you to concentrate on mundane things like pork chops. I thought you'd rather have a meal out—we'll dine out as well this evening if you like.'

'My, my!' Alex marvelled as she allowed a waiter to seat her, and then cast a perfunctory glance over the menu which she was handed. 'Your consideration for your fellow men knows no bounds—or is it that you're afraid I'll dish up a burned offering? Lunch *and* dinner out, you're leading me into the paths of decadence.' And then, because she had been worrying the subject mentally and the waiter had gone off to find a wine list, leaving them alone. 'Ermine has this idea that you supplied the money for our mortgage. It was something the solicitor's clerk said.'

'She's quite right,' he agreed blandly, and ignored her start of surprise. 'Your Mr Dobey approached me when you needed money, and although it couldn't be termed a lucrative investment, at least it was a safe one. He and I worked out the amount you needed and what you could afford to pay.'

'Generous of you!' Alex was vaguely sulky. 'Thank you' was such a difficult thing to say to him, to her despised husband.

'Not at all.' His grin at her was wolfish. 'Like the wicked squire in all those Victorian melodramas—when you fell behind with your payments, I was going to curl my moustache and offer you a way out of your difficulties. Your money or your body! Try the coq au vin,' he advised, 'it's very good.'

'I may as well,' Alex sounded unenthusiastic, 'I don't want a starter, though,' and she lapsed into a brooding silence that lasted all through Greg's soup and halfway through her coq au vin. Her husband was eating trout with almonds, and she wrinkled her nose and wished she had ordered the same, although her chicken dish was very good.

'And what did Ermine want of you this morning?' Greg broke the silence, putting down his fork and looking at her closely, watching every fleeting expression on her face as though he thought she might lie. It annoyed her, and her answer was far more blunt than was her usual wont. She speared a forkful of chicken and contemplated the delicately pink flesh with deep interest.

'She wants to move down to the basement flat, she says it's too noisy on the main floor; people are always walking in and out, it makes her nervous,' and at his raised eyebrow, she added, 'and she asked if we were sleeping together, and I said "Yes", so now she's worried that you'll make me pregnant.'

'And what did you say to calm her fears about the patter of tiny feet?'

Alex chewed, swallowed amd wiped her lips with a napkin. 'I told her not to be so silly.'

'Silly?' Greg refilled her wineglass from the bottle of rosé. 'I shouldn't have thought it silly— after all, it's not beyond the bounds of possibility.'

'It will be from now on,' she answered darkly, and tried to dismiss the subject, but as she told herself later, that was a waste of time. She had presented Greg with a hypothesis and he wouldn't let go until he had worked it out with all its implications.

He ignored her mutter, concentrating on his own thoughts and speaking them slowly, almost hesitantly. He was following through a complicated chain of reasoning, selecting and rejecting possibilities and probabilities.

'A pregnancy wouldn't please your aunt, so you would have two courses of action; you could either stay with me or you could leave me. If you left, again, you'd have a choice; you could have the baby and fight me to keep it or you could give it to me. You see, I've eliminated the possibility of your having an abortion—you wouldn't do that.'

'Give away my child?' Alex glared at her plate. 'I'd never do that either!'

'No, you wouldn't,' and his eyes gleamed with triumph, 'and that leaves me with a handful of trumps. Yes, on mature reflection, it really is a very good idea. Do remind me to thank your aunt for bringing it to my attention.'

'All this is a game to you, isn't it?' There were tears in a lump in her throat and it was painful to speak through them. 'Haven't I enough to worry about? There's Lucy and Ermine and that blasted mortgage, that's enough for any one person without you dragging in a hypothetical baby just to complicate things further. I told you, there isn't going to be one.'

'And I've told you, you worry unnecessarily. Both Lucy and your aunt are quite capable, they're neither of them children. Leave them alone for a while, my dear. You'll find they can manage very well.' Greg paused for a moment as if he was giving some matter his full consideration. 'Do you think you'd like to live in a caravan in Somerset for a few weeks?'

'A caravan? In Somerset?' Disbelief made her voice shrill. She could envisage Greg lounging on a beach in the south of France with a nubile mademoiselle at his side; she could picture him

striding through Rome, browsing in all the
museums, or even yachting in the Bahamas with a
dark-eyed beauty sunbathing in the nude on the
deck, but what he had just suggested seemed
totally out of character. 'Are you out of your tiny
mind, what on earth would I do in a caravan?'

'Oh, we'd find you something to do; how are
you at washing pots?'

Suspicion flickered in her. 'Washing pots?'

Greg seemed amused. 'My darling, there's no
need for you to repeat everything I say like a well
trained parrot,' he slanted a laughing glance at her
flushed face. 'I had a letter from Manny this
morning, I read it in the car while you were doing
your soothing act with your aunt . . .'

'Manny?' she interrupted. 'Who's that?'

'A colleague, an old friend—he used to be my
tutor long ago. He's had permission to open the
site of a Roman villa and he thought I might be
interested. I am, very, so we're going down there
tomorrow.'

'And that's your idea of a holiday?' Alex
wrinkled her nose in distaste. 'I'm not coming with
you.'

His smile became more pronounced. 'Yes, you
are. I'm going, and wheresoever I go, thou goest
also! Since I've re-established my conjugal rights,
I've no intention of letting them lapse again. Cheer
up, my sweet, and give thanks for small mercies.
Manny had a choice of two sites and the other was
in Northumberland! You wouldn't have liked that
a bit, it would have been much too cold and
uncomfortable for you at this time of the year.'

'But Lucy, Ermine . . .?' Greg brushed her

protest aside with the wave of a long finger.

'They'll be all right. They can cope—well, they'll have to, won't they, since you won't be here to coddle them.'

'You're very high-handed,' Alex scowled as she packed a small suitcase before going to bed. Greg was standing over her and giving advice which she didn't want. 'Warm clothes,' he had stipulated, 'and wellingtons—things tend to get muddy, especially if it rains.'

'No wellingtons.' Alex felt rather pleased that she could throw this minute spanner in the works.

He brushed the spanner aside; it was too small to damage his plans. 'We'll get them later.' But he had approved her several pairs of slacks, her woollen skirts and sweaters, reminding her to put in something pretty but not too fussy for the occasional evening when the team would gather at the pub. 'Finished? Good!' He watched as she closed and locked the case. 'Now come to bed.'

'I'm not . . .'

'Yes, you are.' His arm was about her waist and he half dragged, half carried her through to his room. 'Remember what I said about conjugal rights. Stop fighting me, Alexandra, you'll only get hurt, and I don't want to hurt you.'

'It'll be no new thing.' Her face whitened. 'I'm an expert at getting hurt by you, you've done it before. So why be so chary about it now?'

'Then you're used to it.' He looked down into her pale face unsympathetically. 'Come and be hurt, my love. You're a masochist, did you know that? You trot about, looking for the hardest, most painful way of doing things. It shows an alarming lack of self-confidence.'

'I hate you!' she whispered as he stripped off her robe and flower-sprigged cotton nightie and dumped her on the bed. She turned away from him to stare at the wall with wide, unseeing eyes. 'I hate you,' she repeated, but she knew very well he didn't believe her; she didn't believe herself. She knew it wasn't true and her whisper was utterly unconvincing to both of them. 'Please, Greg . . .'

'There's that word again.' He flung himself down beside her and dragged the duvet up to cover them. 'Your timing's astounding, my dear wife,' he was murmuring it in her ear as his hands became seductive. 'You always say it at just the right moment.'

A spry sixty-five-year-old man met them outside the village pub and was introduced as 'Manny, otherwise Mr Emmanuel Gilbert; an old friend. Manny, meet Alexandra, my wife. Move up, darling,' she was told, 'Manny can get in beside you and direct us to the caravan. It'll be a bit of a squeeze, but it's only a short distance, isn't it?'

'About five minutes, Greg, my boy.' Manny scrambled in, clutching a large envelope protectively, and smiled at Alex. 'It's a splendid caravan site, every convenience, mains electricity and drainage, a camp shop—although it isn't open yet, too early in the season. You'll be quite comfortable.'

'Thank you.' Alex forced a smile, and it didn't take much forcing, Manny looked to be a very nice person.

'And of course you'll be quite private,' he gestured with the envelope. 'It's too early in the year for holidaymakers, which is just as well, you can't hide a dig like this and we'd have eager beavers swarming all over the place and doing untold damage.' He smiled at Alex beatifically as though he was personally responsible for their privacy before calling across her to Greg, who was occupied with the narrow road. 'We haven't much time, my boy. The powers that be are going to drive a dual carriageway straight through the site—but wait till we get to your accommodation and I'll show you the crop shadow photographs, they look most promising.'

The caravan was a large and luxurious static. Alex looked approvingly round the small but well equipped kitchenette, the large and comfortable lounge-cum-diner, peeped in at the toilet facilities which included a shower and then inspected the larger of the two bedrooms, which contained a double bed.

'All the comforts of home,' Greg jeered in a whisper as he watched her gaze slide regretfully to the other bedroom, which contained two bunks, placed one above the other. 'No,' he shook his head definitely. 'These look as though they're intended for children, you'd be cramped. Come sleep with me and be my love,' he misquoted. 'Get used to it, Alex, it's going to be your life from now on, and you enjoy it—you know you do.' He kept his voice lowered to an intimate murmur in deference to Manny who, with no further thought for their welfare, had seated himself at the table in the lounge and was spreading out twenty or so blow-ups of pictures of the area taken from a low-flying plane.

'Big, isn't it?' he enthused when Greg took a seat on the other side of the table and Alex busied herself making a pot of tea. She allowed the talk to pass over her head while her own thoughts brought a flush to her face. Greg was right—she did enjoy it; that was the worst part, that she could! That it had become an almost necessary part of her life despite the way he had walked out on her and the things he had done since.

'Bigger than the ones at Nunney and Newton St Loe,' that was Manny being enthusiastic, 'and let's hope, undiscovered so far. It's always such a disappointment when one finds that eighteenth and nineteenth-century fellows have been digging haphazardly with not a thought in their heads but buried treasure.'

'But that's what you're after, surely?' Alex brought the tea to the table and sat down with the men.

'Not at all.' Greg looked at her with indignant grey eyes and then went back to his perusal of the photographs as if they were a blueprint for the Golden Road to Samarkand. 'We're after knowledge, not treasure. The smallest coin with a legible date and inscription is worth as much to us, if not more than all the silver ornaments. Two coins would be better, of course, one at the lowest level so that the earliest date for the building could be established . . .'

'We've pegged it all out,' Manny was still enthusing, 'and I've marked the places on the grid where I think digging would be most fruitful. The

others will be here tonight and I'm hoping for an
early start tomorrow ... Greg, my boy—if the
weather holds out, if it doesn't rain too much—an
inscribed stone—a mosaic in reasonable condition ...' He sighed in gleeful anticipation. 'There
will be eight of us including yourself and your lady
wife—a comfortable number, so we should have
something to show before the road comes and we
have to abandon ...'

'What's this?' Alex had one of the photographs
and was tracing some dark markings on the
ground at some distance from the site of the villa
which stood out clearly as an open-ended rectangle
of lines, too straight and regular to be anything
but man-made. Greg bent his head to study the
photograph more closely.

'Remains of a mediaeval village, I should think.
Possibly abandoned during the Black Death.' He
circled the huddle of tiny markings with his finger.
'A lot of these little places died then.'

'No, not those—these.' Alex pointed to some
much more indistinct and irregular rectangles
which lay at some distance both from the villa and
what might have been a village.

'Early Saxon strip cultivation,' Greg mused over
the wobbly lines and then brightened. 'We may be
in luck, Manny. This could have been the original
Saxon settlement from which the village grew, and
if it was very early, close to the time when the villa
was abandoned or destroyed—you know how the
Saxons disliked and feared buildings made of
stone or brick—they could only have used the villa
site for pasturage, they wouldn't have ploughed it.'

Manny agreed. 'According to the records, that

site has been common land since Domesday, that bears out the theory that the Saxons played safe and kept away from it for fear of offending strange gods. Yes, you're right, Greg—the land would have been used for pasturage only, it may never have been cultivated. If there's anything like six feet of undisturbed soil over the remains, we might find something worthwhile. It's the ploughing that ruins things.'

Alex left them to it and went back to examine the cupboards in the kitchenette. Her presence wasn't necessary. The fridge was spotless and empty except for the remains of the bottle of milk which she had brought with her and had just opened, and the cupboards were in much the same state, so that her box of teabags and packet of sugar looked lonely on the shelves.

'Shopping,' she announced, trying to break in on their conversation, but they didn't even hear her, which was no more than she had expected. She tried again, 'It's a lovely caravan, but there's nothing to eat.'

But the two men remained intent on photographs and maps and she wrinkled her nose in irritation. The state of the commisariat wouldn't bother either Greg or Manny. Manny was lodging at a nearby inn and his meals would be provided, and Greg—she glared at his back from where she was standing. Greg was singleminded, he always had been. For the last few weeks, he had been singlemindedly and ruthlessly pursuing the restoration of his marital relationship, but now he would be devoting the greater part of his energy and massive intellect to the excavation. It wasn't that he didn't care about food, he would simply expect it to appear when he needed it!

Alex wrinkled her brow. She had no magic lamp to rub, there would be no genie to appear at her command laden with eatables and she couldn't drive her husband's car, therefore her only alternative was to insist on being heard before the shops in the nearby small town shut. She marched across to the table. 'Food!' she insisted in a loud voice. 'Even if we have dinner at Manny's inn this evening, we'll still need stuff for the morning,' and she kept her fingers crossed hoping that Greg would spare some part of his physical and mental energies to the getting of supplies, the basic raw materials from which the meals which he would expect to appear could be made.

They dropped Manny off at the pub and inspected the small shop across the village street before going into the little town, where they found a supermarket. 'Things for sandwiches,' Greg directed. 'We'll have a packed lunch each day which we'll eat on site, there won't be time to go back to the caravan. We'll need rolls, apples, biscuits, cans of Coke and beer, things like that.'

'And if it rains? Are we supposed to sit out in a wet field eating soggy sandwiches?'

'We'll take shelter in Manny's travelling workshop,' he grinned at her. 'And thanks for reminding me. If you've found everything you need, we'll go and buy you a pair of wellies. No archaeologist is complete without them! They're more vital than bread and butter.'

By the end of the first week, Alex had got into the

swing of things. Some part of each day she spent in the travelling workshop, which was a conversion from a single-decker bus—she often wondered how an old man like Manny ever managed to drive it, it looked so big and cumbersome. Here, she industriously washed shards of pottery, and when that palled or she ran out of shards, she went on to the site where she was allowed to help by bucketing away the soil excavated from the trenches. Manny, Greg and their five helpers worked away like beavers, and Alex enjoyed watching them, although she was a trifle disappointed that the work she had been given to do was of such a lowly order. She would have liked to dig and find things herself.

Much to everybody's disappointment, the patches of mosaic flooring which had been uncovered showed to be in a very poor state.

'Hypocausts.' Manny took the disappointment well. 'The living rooms had them running under the floors to conduct hot air through from the furnaces—the Roman method of central heating— so the floors rested on brick pillars which have crumbled with time and weight—four or five feet of soil weighs a lot. It's a pity, though, the floor in the atrium looks as though it might have been rather splendid; saltires and interlaced circles in guilloche with a border of lotus leaf scroll. The central medallion could have been imported— we've found a little pile of very small tesserae, much smaller than the ones used by local craftsmen.'

Alex agreed that it was a pity and Manny cheered up. 'We'd have had to cover it again even if it had been in good condition, we don't have enough time to lift anything like that. But the tesselated pavements in the colonnades have survived, although the work is very rudimentary, blue and white diagonal stripes, nothing fancy.' He became grandfatherly. 'Ask your husband about it, child. He's the expert on mosaics,' and his eyes twinkled. 'It's good to have him back working in England again, you know. Britain might only have been an outpost of the Empire, but it still has a lot to offer,' and he darted off in answer to a muffled cry from the bottom of a nearby trench.

Alex knew a bit about mosaics, hadn't she typed out a whole book that Greg had written on the subject *and* indexed all the photographs and drawings that illustrated the text? But although she knew a little, she was no expert, and she was hesitant about showing her ignorance among a company which seemed to be so very well informed. Greg, however, knew just how abysmally ignorant she was, so she could ask him questions.

'The mosaics here—are they from the Dorchester centre?'

'Looks like it.' Greg raised an eyebrow at her. 'Are you beginning to find it interesting or are you trying to divert my attention away from that pan of burned sausages?'

'I wasn't diverting anything, and the sausages aren't burned,' she protested. 'I was trying to show an interest, but if you don't want . . .'

'You're bored with washing pottery fragments, I suppose.'

'A bit,' she admitted as she creamed the

potatoes. 'It isn't what you'd call an inspired occupation . . .'

'And you'd prefer to be where the action's at.' He raised a humorous eyebrow.

'It would be more exciting.' Alex halted while she added more butter to the potatoes and marshalled her thoughts into some sort of order. 'Anybody can wash bits of pot and put them in plastic bags.'

'Precisely.' He came to look over her shoulder at her preparations for their evening meal. 'Anybody! That's why you've been entrusted with the job. You're allowing an experienced person to get on with more important work. You wouldn't like it anyway, there's not much glamour or romance in sitting in a trench digging out more bits of pottery and sticking little markers in to show where each find came from.'

'All right,' she sighed grudgingly, 'I won't complain. I'll wash your bits of pot and I'll empty buckets full of soil . . .'

'That's my good girl!' and Alex told herself tartly that Greg's good humour came of getting his own way about everything—but it was a real if lazy good humour and quite a pleasant thing to live with. Later after the meal, he came to sit beside her on the banquette and there was the feel of his thigh against hers and his arm about her waist.

'Enjoying the break?'

Alex retreated swiftly into her cool shell. He was disturbing her again and it was important to her that he shouldn't realise it.

'Thank you, yes. It's all been very pleasant and instructive. Would you like a cup of tea or coffee? I can easily . . .'

'To hell with tea and coffee!' The arm about her tightened and she trembled slightly. 'You know what I want and I know what you want. Let's go to bed.'

She closed her eyes, opened her mouth and listened to what she was saying. Only the first part of it was what she intended, after that the words came out of their own volition or as if some other woman, not herself, was saying them.

'You have no delicacy! And yes, I think an early night would be a good idea—working out of doors all day, I get very sleepy.'

'Too tired?' Greg nuzzled at a point just behind her ear.

'No,' said that other woman inside Alex, and she gave a soft chuckle. 'Not that tired!'

Alex emptied the last load of dirt from her bucket and straightened her aching back. Two things about this dig would remain for ever in her mind. Buckets of dirt were very heavy and washing pots in cold water made her hands swell so that her wedding ring was cutting into her flesh. But she had enjoyed it all, and it was with regret that she left the site and walked back in the pale spring sunlight to the caravan, where she would start on preparations for a meal.

Nearly two weeks of forgetfulness and absence of worry had brought about a big improvement in her. She felt better and she looked better, there was some colour in her cheeks and her slacks and skirts were becoming decidedly tight. It was wrong of her to deliberately close her mind to Ermine's need of her, to cast aside her perpetual worry about Lucy, but she couldn't help it. For the first time in years, she felt free, and she was enjoying it.

All the other people on the dig had been kind and companionable, they'd never made her feel like a moron, and the evenings when they'd all gathered in the pub, playing darts or dominoes, had been fun. Greg had dispensed with his suave, well dressed look and had become almost ordinary, looking just like one of the others in what seemed to be a uniform for hardworking archaeologists—stained grey flannels, stained grey shirt with the sleeves rolled up to the elbows, an ancient pullover, liberally smeared with soil and mud, a waterproof nylon jacket, ripped in several places, and a pair of big, clumpy boots.

This had been the last day at the site and she had at last got her wish and been relieved of pot washing. She and Greg had spent most of the day at the bottom of a wide trench, sandpapering a corner of a mosaic floor. As Greg pointed out, the sandpapering didn't hurt, it improved; it brought back the original colour to the small pieces of stone and chalk which made up the complicated design, making it live again if only for a short while.

When they had done and the stone chips glowed white, black, grey and various shades of pink and red, Manny would come with his camera to make a permanent record of what they had found, and then the soil would be shovelled back into the trench and the handiwork of some long-dead Romano-British artist would once more be covered from view, perhaps for ever. It was a pity really, after all the hard work which had gone into uncovering it, but as Greg had said, nowadays roads were more important than relics, as any Roman would have understood.

'Practicality,' he had pointed out. 'That was the motivating force of the Empire. They didn't indulge in romanticism and they weren't artists, not in the modern sense. They were practical engineers. They had a blueprint to run everything from a town council to an empire and they never let sentiment get in their way.'

'You're a bit of a Roman yourself,' Alex sniffed. 'You work to a blueprint and there isn't a speck of romance about you.' The look she gave him was almost a glare. 'The only thing that matters to you is what *you* think!'

'But I'm usually right,' he said with a self-satisfied grin that made the hairs on her neck rise. 'I had a wife who wouldn't live with me, she thought she'd be unhappy, so I forced her and she found she quite liked it. You do, don't you? Your trouble, my dear, is that you're too much of a romantic; you wanted a "parfit gentil knight", and that species doesn't exist, Chaucer invented it. Everybody has failings, you have yours and I have mine. I'm willing to live with your bad points and I don't ask you to overlook mine. Just add them up, subtract them from the pleasure we get from each other and you'll find the balance is on the credit side.'

'That's not love,' she muttered, half to herself, but he heard her and burst into a roar of laughter which caused curious eyes to peep at them from the lip of the trench.

'It's marriage, my dear. That's what it's all about.'

'I don't agree.' Alex bent over her bit of mosaic to hide her embarrassment and scrubbed viciously with her sandpaper at an unoffensive section of scrollwork. 'I don't see that I have so many bad points for you to overlook.'

'Careful, my love!' and Greg's eyes glittered with amusement while his mouth curled into a devastating smile that made her heart thump heavily. 'You're sounding smug. Your worst failing is that you don't devote yourself completely to me, I have to take second or third place to your sister and your aunt, neither of whom need you, although they go through the motions of wanting you from time to time.'

'They do need me,' she objected. 'You don't, you don't need anybody. You can hire a typist, employ a housekeeper and buy a woman for the night-time. You've done all those things before, why change the pattern?'

Greg's lashes came down to conceal his eyes while his face assumed an expression of great virtue. 'I've done those things before, as you say, but you must remember, I'm not a bachelor any more. I found a very good typist—you—and you're a good housekeeper as well, not to mention your performance in bed, which is without equal in my experience, so you fit the bill for all three positions. Think of the money I'm saving! I get the work done satisfactorily *and* all the home comforts for a fraction of what it used to cost me.'

Alex flushed. 'You're turning into a miser,' she hedged, wishing they'd never got on to this subject and desperately trying to think of some way to change it.

'Mmm, and virtuous with it!' His amusement increased. 'It saves me a lot of mental effort. No more "Miss—er" to the typist or housekeeper and only one name to remember when we wake in the mornings. It's an ideal situation, and all for the cost of a marriage licence.'

'You're laughing at me,' she accused.

'Of course I'm laughing at you, my part blind little wife. Stop wriggling like a fish on the end of a line—you like the situation just as much as I do, but you're not honest enough to admit it. If it wasn't for me, you'd be marching about from office to office in your Mary Poppins grey uniform and being unfulfilled. I don't like to think of you denying yourself fulfilment and I know you'd never accept it unless it was all very proper. But since we're married, you can wake up every morning feeling just as virtuous as I do.'

'You feel virtuous? I don't believe it!' Alex snorted down her small, straight nose. 'You don't know what virtue means!'

'But I do.' Greg reached across and took her hand, removing the sandpaper and holding it warmly. 'Virtue is living with my wife, quarrelling with her, making love to her . . .'

'And how long will that last?' she asked sardonically.

'That's up to you, my dear.' He gave her an enigmatic look. 'Maybe, with a bit of luck and a lot of hard work, it could last the rest of our lives. All you have to remember is that I come first and that I'm not sharing with anybody.'

CHAPTER EIGHT

GREG drove them back to Kensington through rain which was pouring down from a leaden sky, and Alex huddled in her seat and looked out at the weather gloomily. She should have been overjoyed, as were the rest of the team, that the rain had held off for two weeks, but she was filled with a sense of foreboding and it showed.

'Not looking forward to going back?' That was Greg as he peered through the murk, and he seemed almost pleased about it.

'Not much,' she admitted, and then, as an excuse, 'the weather . . .'

'Not the weather.' He was definite. 'You're a born martyr, but you don't enjoy it. You've suddenly started worrying about your sister and aunt, and after a fortnight or so free from them, it's getting you down.'

Alex ignored him. Who was he to set himself up as an expert on psycho-analysis? The dig had been roughly filled in so that everything was covered in situ and there was no danger of a sheep or cow breaking a leg in the little time left to them before the road makers came, and Manny had driven off in his converted bus, looking like an aged leprechaun and gloating over his boxes of shards and a pile of film to be developed and printed.

Alex knew she was going to miss the dig, miss Manny cavorting about behind his camera and flashgun, miss the company and the pleasant evenings in the pub—she thought she might even miss the interminable bowls of water and pieces of broken pot. After a few days with them, she had been able to sort them out, carefully putting on one side the bits of fine red Samian ware, so thin and hard it was almost metallic, and separating them from the coarse black earthenware.

There had been a preponderance of the coarse stuff; evidently the finer, imported pottery was used only by the small family in the villa, the servants and slaves had made do with less expensive dishes and beakers—so people didn't change much in sixteen hundred years! She herself could just remember when her mother only used china for the family and the daily woman was expected to drink her tea out of earthenware.

The haul from the dig hadn't been very large. There were all the marvellous photographs, but apart from them, it hadn't amounted to much. A few coins, a small green glass vial, some pieces of withered leather, a piece of stone with a Chi Rho inscribed on it—which Greg said showed that somebody practised Christianity—and the bags full of potsherds. The biggest find, in size, was a battered and noseless stone head of Janus with two faces, one in the front and one looking backwards, so the old gods hadn't been completely abandoned or banished with the advent of the new religion.

Alex equated that old god with her love for Greg. That too had been a battered and buried thing, chipped and defaced, but in spite of all her efforts to banish it, it remained, and it would now, she knew, endure for the rest of her life. It was against all sense and reason, but it still existed and it refused to be denied. Almost as though her burial of it for three years had simply served to make it stronger and more enduring. It would bring her heartache, but she thought she might, just might be able to draw enough honey from it to sweeten the bitter, lonely days to come.

With an attempt at humour, although her mood was like the weather, wet and depressing, she turned as she dropped her coat on the hall table.

'What's to do now, have I to start typing at last?'

'Tomorrow you can make a start on my rough notes of the dig.' Greg had picked up the little scatter of letters which had been lying on the mat and was shuffling through them. 'That's as far as we'll go for the moment—anything more will have to wait until we get the photographs from Manny, and my book can wait as well. I owe Manny this dig.' His fingers selected one envelope, a large buff-coloured one, and he handed it to her. 'Something from your agency? You can tell them that you're no longer in the market, you're fully employed. What's more, I'm very satisfied with your performance so far—and you haven't started typing yet!'

'There are times when I could hit you,' Alex said darkly and with a threatening scowl as she tossed the envelope down on top of her coat. 'I'll see to it later, no time now,' and she shivered as she turned on the central heating before she went fishing in the freezer for something for dinner. Steak—she pawed around and emerged with two packets which she opened and set to thaw while she decided there was a good hour and a half before she need start preparations for a meal. Time for a lovely bath, a luxury she had been denied in the caravan—showers were all very well, they were quick and refreshing, but there was no substitute for a bath, for the hedonistic delight of wallowing up to her chin in hot, scented water. She wanted to do it and she wanted to do it now!

She indulged herself for nearly half an hour before, in response to repeated knockings on the bathroom door, she reluctantly hauled herself out of the water, wrapped herself in a large bathsheet, opened the door a few inches and put her head through the very narrow gap.

'What's the matter?'

Greg squinted past her, into the steam-laden room, and then looked back again at her heat-flushed face and damp shoulders, grinning at her diabolically.

'Little pig, hogging the bathroom like that. Do you think nobody else lives here?'

'Sorry,' but she wasn't in the least bit sorry. 'You should get yourself a separate shower, some people like to wallow undisturbed.' She caught sight of a pile of garments slung over his arm. 'What's that?'

'Cleaning.' He demonstrated the clothing he'd worn on the dig. 'You'd better make up a load and deliver them tomorrow morning.'

'Mmm.' She made no concessions, the bathroom door was firmly held against her foot. 'The soil of Somerset is rich and brown, and when wet, it goes a long way. I've smears of it all over most of my things, including a couple of cashmere sweaters.'

She turned back and shut the door firmly in his face to wriggle her still damp body into her robe and belt it firmly about her waist before she stepped out into the passsage. 'Give, oh, Master.' She relieved him of the garments, wrinkling her nose in distaste at their condition. 'I'll stuff everything into a couple of carriers and offload at the cleaner's first thing tomorrow morning.'

'Obedient little thing,' Greg marvelled.

'Not at all.' The bath had restored her good humour and she smiled acidly. 'Write me down as efficient—obedience was never one of my strong points!' and she swished off, leaving him standing by the bathroom door.

Back in the privacy of her own room, she unearthed a couple of carrier bags from the wardrobe and started to make a mental list. Three pairs trousers, men's—four pairs slacks, lady's—eight assorted sweaters—one tweed coat, lady's—and she went down the passage to the hall table to fetch it, picking up the envelope at the same time. Back with the pile of cleaning, she rooted in her bag for a ballpoint and started to make a rough list on the back of the buff envelope. Half way through, she stopped and turned the envelope over. Of course it wasn't from the agency, they used a long white one with the name and address embossed on the flap; besides, this address was scrawled in Lucy's writing. It was probably the photographs taken at the engagement party, it felt excitingly thick, and with eager fingers she ripped it open.

There were no photographs, just two letters and a covering note from her sister. 'Alex, I found these. Please don't ask where. But they're addressed to you and I thought you should have them. Love, Lucy'.

Alex raised her eyebrows and turned her attention to the letters. They were both from Greg and neither had been opened—but the dates! The first had been posted soon after he had arrived alone in New York on what was to have been their honeymoon, and she dealt with that one first, opening it and reading his black, clear handwriting. Greg had written tersely, as though he was out of patience with her. He hoped she had come to her senses and he would wait in New York for a further week for her to join him. He enclosed her airline ticket which she should take to a travel agent in order to get a reservation on a later flight—and the signature was 'Greg', just that and no more, no Love, not even Sincerely.

Raged boiled up in her. How dared he have written to her like this! As though she was some slave to come running when he raised his finger but—on the other hand, he *had* written, he hadn't given up straight away. All the same, it was just as well she'd never received this letter. He would wait for her, would he? He would give her a week! It wasn't a letter at all, it was an ultimatum!

Alex pushed the single sheet and the out-of-date airline ticket and reservation back into the envelope and opened the second letter. This one had an Italian stamp and had been posted just over a year ago. Once again, Greg had been terse but oh, so polite. They had been apart for nearly two years and he could see no further point in continuing the relationship. He was sure that it must be as much a bore to her as it was to him. He had taken the liberty of forwarding to his solicitor all the details of the information she would require in order to obtain a divorce. He had attached the name and address of the solicitor so that she could get in touch without delay, and this time, the signature wasn't even 'Greg', it was a formal 'G. Mallus', as if she was no more than a brief acquaintance!

With shaking fingers, Alex returned the letter to its envelope and then, on legs that felt as though they were made of rubber, she crossed to the dressing table and put both letters away in a little-used drawer, hiding them under a few chiffon scarves which she didn't like. She closed the drawer firmly and then went back to sit on the edge of the bed and try to stop shivering.

From the other bedroom she could hear Greg moving about. There was the noise of his wardrobe door being opened, the rattle of hangers on the metal rail, the opening and shutting of drawers, and over all these sounds, a soft whistling could be heard, melodious and carefree. Alex lowered her head into her hands and stuffed her fingers into her ears. Nothing made any sense any more. Greg had wanted a divorce, yet here he was now, playing the part of a quite satisfied husband. It wasn't like him to change his mind.

She raised her head and stared at the wall which divided the two bedrooms as though, if she stared hard enough, it would vanish and she would be able to see him, to see what he was thinking, what his expression was when she wasn't there. And her mind went on sorting through its store of information, but only one fact kept hammering away in her head. Greg had wanted a divorce— Over a year ago he'd practically asked for one, and she'd not known and had done nothing about it.

Perhaps he had wanted to remarry, perhaps the woman had grown tired of waiting for him to be free—perhaps she'd left him to marry somebody else——

And the letters—Lucy said she had 'found' them, but one didn't lose letters! They must have been kept from her, but Greg wouldn't know that. He would have thought she'd received them and ignored them. She *would* have ignored the first one, but the second—that was a different matter! If he had wanted to marry somebody else, she would have wished him every happiness and done everything possible to free him, she loved him too much to be a dog in the manger. If happiness for him was another woman, another wife, she wouldn't have kept him tied to her.

Her mind went back again—the letters had been kept from her, hidden away, and Lucy had found them, which meant only one thing, and she cringed from the thought. Ermine had taken them—but why? To keep her niece and Greg apart? If only her aunt had known! She hadn't kept them apart at all. In a way, she had brought them back together again. But Ermine wouldn't have known that; she hadn't opened the letters, only hidden them.

Alex seized on a faint thread of hope. Maybe it hadn't been Ermine, maybe the letters had been truly lost. She held on to that thought until common sense and reason told her it was ridiculous. One lost letter, maybe, but two, and so long between them—no, it was impossible. Once more the pain of her aunt's duplicity spread through her, so that when Greg came into her room she raised her head and looked at him with pain-filled eyes.

'Aren't you dressed yet?' He looked at the damp robe which she was still wearing. 'Hurry up, my dear.' And then, 'Aren't you well? You look ghastly.' His fingers came to touch her forehead, which was icy cold and clammy with perspiration.

'A bit of a chill, I think.' Her voice was husky and she strove to keep it as normal as possible. Greg must know nothing of this until she'd had a chance to talk to her sister and her aunt, after she'd done that would be plenty of time to make decisions. 'I'll see to dinner for you and have an early night. I'll be better in the morning.'

'Into bed with you now.' He was irritable and ignored her wriggling as he stripped the damp robe from her numbed body and dropped her nightdress over her head. 'At once, and don't bother about dinner, I'll get something sent in.' He switched on the electric blanket and bundled her into bed without ceremony. 'A hot drink and a couple of aspirin, that should do it. You choose the most inconvenient times to catch cold, don't you? You know we're going to be busy.'

Alex watched his retreating back and breathed a sigh of relief when the door closed behind him. She was now trembling from shock and her teeth were chattering. All she wanted was to be alone, to shut her eyes and try to exorcise the dirty little trails in her mind. But when she closed her eyes, the second letter was there in the darkness behind her eyelids, and the words stood out in letters of fire so that she read it over and over again. With a gasp, she opened her eyes and scrambled out of bed just as Greg entered with the promised tea.

'Back to bed,' he ordered.

'No,' she defied him. 'It's nothing worth bothering about. I've never coddled myself and I'm not starting now. Thanks,' as he put the cup and saucer down on the bedside table and added the aspirin bottle from the bathroom cabinet. 'Now, if you'll go, I'll get dressed.'

'I'd rather you stayed in bed, at least until tomorrow morning.'

'No!' She knew she was overreacting as the word escaped her lips violently. 'I loathe staying in bed, it's boring. I'll be much better doing someting. Oh, for heaven's sake get out of here, stop hovering like an old hen! I want to dress and I can't bear being watched.' It all came out as an irritable snap, waspish and stinging. 'Or aren't I entitled to that much privacy?' But her last sally was addressed to the blank panels of the bedroom door which he had closed behind him as he departed with an exasperated growl.

Alex dragged on some underwear and a new skirt and topped it with a cashmere twinset. Not the most suitable garments for a quiet dinner at home, she looked rather as though she was ready for a hike over the heath, but she was shivering again and even the two layers of wool didn't warm her. Her reflection in the mirror was far from reassuring, there was no colour in her face and her eyes looked bruised. A little make-up helped, but not much, and while she was applying it and brushing her hair into order, she turned everything over in her mind.

She supposed the most sensible thing to do would be to get the letters out of the drawer, take them in to Greg, wherever he was, toss them carelessly into his lap and say, 'Look what I've just received!'—make some jokey comment about the post becoming slower and slower, but she couldn't do it. It was too important a thing to be treated lightly.

The first thing to do was to see Lucy, and when she had done that and made sure of her suspicions—what should she do then? Go and see her aunt, she supposed, and after that—go away. Write Greg a letter apologising, explaining—that would be best! It was funny, damned funny, so funny that it made her cry. Tears were a painful lump in her throat. She hadn't wanted to live with him again, and now she would have given anything she possessed not to have to leave him. But he had asked for a divorce, he hadn't got it, so he'd evidently decided to make the best of what he had. That would be why he was so horribly practical about everything, it wasn't that he was emulating his damned Romans, it was because it was the only way he could approach this disastrous marriage.

In the kitchen, her hands were busy, but it didn't stop her thinking. She grilled the steaks, made a sauce from a can of creamed mushrooms, fried potato chips and boiled frozen peas. It wouldn't be an inspired meal, but anything more complicated was beyond her at the moment. She solved the sweet problem with a bottle of preserved peaches and a bowl of yoghurt, feeling rather surprised that she hadn't burned, spilled or dropped anything, and spread the cheeseboard with a virulent-looking Dorset Blue Vinny cheese which she had brought back with her from a visit to Sherborne. It looked offputting in its blue-veined splendour, and she left it on the counter where she couldn't smell it. Greg had said he liked it and she had bought some, but now she wished she hadn't. It reminded her of the letters, it looked old and better buried.

'Feeling any better?' Greg studied her face as she pushed her steak round the plate. He was being sympathetic—at least, it had started that way, but he refused to understand why she wanted to be alone that night.

'I've a screaming headache,' she snapped, 'and I don't suppose I'll sleep much. I'll only disturb you.'

'Have some whisky,' he advised callously, his sympathy evaporating like snow in summer, but Alex shuddered at the thought. Her mind had absorbed the shock, but nausea had settled in the pit of her stomach so that the idea of whisky made her want to vomit. She shook her head, abandoned her fruitless attempt to eat anything and dragged herself back to her bedroom, carefully locking the doors before she scrambled into bed.

What little sleep she had was made hideous with dreams and she woke to a grey dawn feeling more exhausted than if she'd sat up all night. The dolphin clock said it was half past five, and as it ticked away the seconds and minutes she lay watching the slow movement of the hands around the dial while she made her plans.

The first thing was to go to the branch of her bank in Kensington, get a new cheque book and provide herself with some ready money. After that, she would go and see Lucy, maybe have lunch with her. Then she would say whatever had to be said to Ermine, and after that, she would go. She wondered how much a ticket to Outer Mongolia would cost, or perhaps Timbuctoo—but then there would be all the bother of passports and foreign currency—her eyelids drooped and the next time she looked at the clock, it told her it was nearly nine.

She took a hurried shower, scrambled into some outdoor clothing, gave her face a flick with some powder and screwed up her hair into a tight, neat pleat at the back of her head, then she walked down to the kitchen with an air of calm which belied the tight cramp in her stomach. At least today she would be doing something; inactivity was making things worse.

Greg was before her, the table was partly laid and the aroma of fresh coffee greeted her nostrils as she opened the door.

'A quick recovery!' He raised a disbelieving eyebrow as though she might have been faking.

'Fear!' Alex riposted swiftly. Whatever happened, he must not suspect anything. 'I hear you in the kitchen and I never know what to expect—a conflagration with burned offerings on the side or you, flat on your back and dead of electrocution.'

'You sound better, more like your acid little self,' he remarked admiringly. 'But you still look pale. Go back to bed and I'll get the doctor to call.'

'And leave you to burn the place down? No, thank you.' She pushed past him to get at the toaster which, after a thorough cleaning and a bang in the right place with a wooden spoon, was now working perfectly. 'Besides, I *am* better. I expect it was all that steam and bath oil last evening, it must have affected my sinuses, like hay fever.'

'And I was so looking forward to playing the part of a caring husband!' Greg's face creased in a grin so that the lines from his nose to his mouth deepened. 'I was going to bring you tempting morsels on a tray, change your sweat-soaked sheets, give you a blanket bath—all practice for when you're pregnant. Are you?'

'Certainly not!' Alex kept her head turned away from him. 'Whatever gave you that idea?'

'I don't have the idea, some rudimentary mental arithmetic rules it out, but I'm not displeased. We need a lot more time to ourselves before we start on a family.' He became sententious. 'Children are a responsibility. For instance, we'd have to find another place to live—a flat's no place for a baby. We'd need a house and a garden, somewhere out in the country. St Albans is a nice spot. I've been looking at a few advertisements, but I haven't seen anything suitable yet, and in any case, I'd like you to see Leptis Magna, Rome and Timgad before you become a mother, not to mention places like Nimes and Arles; the aqueduct at Nimes is a masterpiece of engineering and the Maison Carré—it used to be a temple . . .'

Alex went on making toast and let his words flow over her head; she had other things to think about, and she only returned her attention when he was concluding, '. . . But I admit I'm disappointed. Every man likes to think he's virile enough for that. Are you sure it isn't your fault?'

'Wishful thinking,' Alex said tartly, and breathed a sigh of relief as the toaster popped. The nerves in her stomach had tightened so that the nausea came again to set her perspiring. Didn't she have enough to worry about without contemplating an unwanted pregnancy—but was it really unwanted? It was a question she shied away from, putting it firmly to the back of her mind, only it wouldn't stay there.

'Fool!' Alex cursed herself as she stuffed toast in the rack and searched for a fresh jar of marmalade. She'd never bothered about precautions, never even thought about them, and heaven knew it was easy enough nowadays. A baby would be the last straw. Marriage was a tie which could be broken, but a baby would be a complication, and that was putting it mildly. No way would Greg let her keep it, not if they were divorced, and no way would she give it up . . . They'd be tied together in this bond of practicality he called marriage and she would never be able to set him free. And all the while, a jeering little voice in her head was saying, 'But you don't want to set him free, that's why you've so conveniently forgotten about precautions. You want to stay here and love him for as long as he'll let you.' But she didn't allow any of this to show on her face or in her voice.

'Let's stop talking about fanciful things, improbable things. I've a lot to do this morning, so I'll have to rush off.' She drained her coffee cup at one go and prepared to rise. 'There's that huge pile of cleaning, it weighs a ton.'

'Order a taxi,' Greg advised, 'and while you're out, get something done about your finger.'

'My finger?'

'Mmm.' He leaned across and touched her left hand. 'You've been wincing a bit, I've noticed,' he picked up her hand and inspected the third finger closely. 'That ring's too tight, it's stopping the circulation.'

'And whose fault is that, who was so damn satisfied it was so tight? Who said I'd have a job to get it off? Who forced it on? I didn't want it, I said so at the time, remember?' Alex was nearly in tears, so many things were coming down on her all at once and she didn't think she could stand any more. 'It's you,' she muttered. 'You're to blame for everything, you and your high-handed ways. I've a lot of shopping to do, and if I have to see about this ring, I don't know when I'll be back.' She poured herself another cup of coffee while she tried to control mounting hysteria.

'What about lunch?' Greg remained calm even though she was provoking him, she could see that by the way his brows had come down in a solid black bar across his eyes. Who cared? Let him stew!

'There's some sliced ham in the fridge,' she snapped, abandoning her coffee. 'Make yourself a sandwich!' And she stormed out of the kitchen.

It was twelve o'clock before she emerged from the bank with her new cheque book and a comforting reserve of cash. She had dumped the cleaning and waited patiently while the girl had made out the list, giving her a separate receipt for each article, and then she had gone to the jewellers and demanded haughtily that the ring be removed. And 'No,' she had glared at the sycophantic young man who had been impressed by the mink coat, she didn't want another ring. 'Just get it off,' she told him crossly.

Did Madam realise it would have to be cut? Madam did, and in her present mood, she didn't care if they cut the finger off with it, although she didn't say so but sat impatiently while the ring was sawn off from her finger, and she accepted the pieces, which were put carefully in a small box for her, with a bad grace. She had thought she would feel better when it was gone, but no such thing, and she put this down to the fact that the large buff envelope containing Greg's two letters was reposing in her handbag. She hadn't liked to leave it at the flat, she didn't want Greg to see it, not until she could present him with a fait accompli, and it would have been so easy for him to find it by accident—he looked in the most curious places for pencils and ballpoint pens.

After a great deal of crossing and recrossing London, she found herself in what Lucy called the Flower Power shop, and this was one place where a surly voice and an unpleasant manner wouldn't serve her purpose, so her face was bland and her voice honeyed as she gently persuaded the manageress to allow Lucy to take an early lunch.

'What gives?' Lucy stared at her sister across the small table in the nearby restaurant. 'Alex, you're behaving out of character. I'm the one who's always wangling time off.'

Alex stared down at the red chequered tablecloth and waited until the waitress had departed with their order, and then, with a hurried glance around to be sure they were not observed, she withdrew the envelope from her handbag.

'This!'

'Oh.' Lucy looked uncomfortable. 'Look, Alex, it was none of my business, and looking back, I'm not sure I should have sent them to you, but they were your letters and I thought at the time that you should have them.' She raised clear blue eyes and looked straight into Alex's grey green ones. 'I didn't hide them from you.'

'Then it was Ermine,' said Alex with a snap. 'Have you read them?'

'Certainly not!' Lucy was indignant. 'How could I, they hadn't been opened. But has it put things right for you and Greg?'

Alex shook her head mournfully. 'No, it hasn't. It's just confused everything even further. I was in enough of a stew before, but after this, I don't know which way is up.'

'Sorry,' Lucy said sympathetically. 'This is what comes of interfering, I suppose. First Ermine collaring your letters and hiding them from you and then me finding them while I was helping her move her things down to the basement flat. I'm sorry, Alex, honestly I am. I thought I was doing you a favour, making everything right for you. I thought Greg would have written that he loved you for ever and ever, and then you'd fall into his arms and things would end with an orchestra playing while you both walked hand in hand into the sunset, like they do in films. And it isn't like that?' She sounded disappointed.

'Not a bit like that.' Alex was firm and tried to keep the sadness out of her voice. 'I shall have to see Ermine, of course. I can't think why she should have done such a thing.'

'You can't think? Oh, Alex, our little aunty has been up to her tricks, trying to break you and Greg up, that's all,' Lucy growled, and her eyes sparkled with temper. 'She's a bitch—I've tried to tell you often enough, but you'd never believe me. Hey, drink that coffee, you look as though you need it. You're not going to faint, are you?'

'No.' Alex pulled herself together. 'But it's made everything so much worse. I didn't know what to do before, but now I can't even think straight. If I'd had those letters straight away, things wouldn't be in such an appalling tangle—and if it hadn't been Ermine who kept them from me . . .'

'Well, it was, and you can't change it,' said Lucy practically. 'Don't go to Kensington, Alex, go home and tell Greg about it, let him deal with it. He'll hit the roof, and after that I hope he'll hit Aunty. Or if you're set on going, let me come with you.'

'No, love, I'll manage this on my own.' Alex pushed aside her untouched plate and waited while Lucy poured another cup of coffee. 'I thought— oh, I don't know what I thought, that's why I didn't tell Greg about the letters. In the second one, he suggested I divorce him. I expect he'd found somebody else.'

'Who wouldn't?' Lucy snorted as she passed over the filled cup. 'You turned him loose, and he's only a man, after all, not a plaster saint. Three years is a long time . . .'

'Quite a woman of the world!' This time Alex's smile was a real one. 'You constantly surprise me, I keep forgetting you've grown up.'

Lucy looked wise. 'You've never noticed, same as you never noticed how Aunty ran our lives. There've been times when I wanted to shake you, you've been so blind. But don't worry, I'll not say a word about this to Robert, it might get back to his mother and then I'd really be up the creek. I've been learning a few things about her, you know, and she isn't half as bad as I thought. I think she might even have accepted the sister of a girl who had one broken marriage behind her, but I know she wouldn't accept this—one of my relatives who interfered with the Establishment to the extent of pinching the Royal Mail! That would make me kin to a criminal and quite outside the pale.' She returned to the attack. 'I still think I should come with you, you're so soft!'

'Not any more.' Alex finished her coffee and called for the bill, pushing some notes across to her sister. 'Get yourself a sweet, and don't hurry. I'm going now, but I'll let you know how I get on. I'll check first and then, if we're right, it's going to be dignified—and that, my infant, you're not.'

'I never pretended to be.' Lucy's little plump hand came to rest on her sister's arm, preventing her from rising. 'If Aunty gets on her high horse, promise me you won't lay back your ears and bolt for cover like a frightened rabbit.'

Alex registered surprise. 'Is that how I seem to you, a frightened bunny? I've just admitted I don't know a lot about you, but you don't know me either, not if you think that's how I'd behave. I suppose what it comes down to is that we neither of us knows the other as well as we should. I apologise, and I promise we'll do better in the future.'

'We do already,' Lucy grinned. 'You're much more human since you went back to Greg, and he's marvellous, almost like a real brother.' Her voice sharpened. 'And you won't be a rabbit— promise, you won't let her shout you down.'

'Ermine doesn't shout,' Alex objected.

'Fat lot you know,' Lucy said crudely. 'Wait for me while I pay the bill and I'll come with you to the Underground—and may I keep the change, please, I'm very short this week.'

CHAPTER NINE

IT was nice to know what other people thought of one. Alex sat in the train and thought about it. Lucy thought she was weak because she hadn't fought with Ermine, Ermine had thought she was weak but for a different reason, Ermine would have liked her to dragoon her younger sister into a pattern which that sister would never have fitted. And Greg thought . . . no, she didn't know exactly what Greg thought, except that he objected to what he called her running around after her sister and her aunt.

But she wasn't weak, not really. She didn't interfere, that was all. As she said, she only stood on the sidelines and picked up the pieces when necessary. All the same, these few weeks away from her family had taught her a lot. She'd learned that Lucy was no longer a child and that Ermine could get on very well without her. What was more, she'd learned that Greg could be a very good—no, a superlative husband when he put his mind to it, and until yesterday she had hoped he'd put his mind to it for a very long time. She descended from the train realising that her bit of situation analysis had served one purpose at least, it had stopped her thinking about the coming interview with her aunt.

Alex let herself into the basement flat with her own key and wondered whether Ermine would be annoyed that she still had it. And she wasn't being weak or frightened about that either. It was simply a matter of principle. She wouldn't have liked anybody to have a duplicate key to the place where she was living, but on the other hand, she could hardly wait on the doorstep for a couple of hours until Ermine came home from the office.

The basement flat felt chill and smelled very strongly of lavender polish, everything was ultra-tidy and neat, and as Alex peeped into one room after the other, her eyebrows rose.

She noticed that Ermine had taken over the bedroom which she herself had used, and Ermine had banished the duvet with its flower-sprigged cotton cover as well as the matching curtains. In their place was thick rich yellow velvet, and Alex wrinkled her nose at it. She had used cotton for ease of washing, this heavy stuff would collect dust and have to be cleaned. Ermine should know better.

All her aunt's things had been brought down here, the ornaments, the framed photographs, small pieces of furniture—a little desk and some stools had been crowded into the lounge area and Ermine's favourite pictures now adorned the walls. Lucy's beanbag seat had been banished; their aunt had always frowned upon it, saying it was an inelegant form of seating. Perhaps she'd made Lucy take it with her.

Quietly, Alex filled the kettle and switched it on in preparation for a cup of something hot, and she switched on the heating. If she sat around at the present temperature, she would be frozen stiff by the time her aunt returned from work. As for the

cup of something hot, she reflected that it would
be wiser to get it now because after she had said
what had to be said to Ermine, she would be lucky
if her aunt didn't throw the teapot at her. She
wasn't looking forward to the meeting, but it had
to come, and while she was waiting for the kettle
to boil, she forced herself to relax. There was over
an hour to wait and she hitched a stool up to the
kitchen counter and made herself comfortable.

Maybe there was a quite logical explanation for
what her aunt had done, and Alex held on to this
hope because despite Lucy's story and in spite of
her own convictions, she was still hoping for some
sort of miracle. She remembered Ermine with
affection. They had been very close, more like
sisters than niece and aunt, she had been closer to
Ermine than to her own sister, although she now
realised that this had been her own fault as much
as anybody's. Lucy had never seemed to need her
as Ermine had. Lucy had always been so
independent, so self-sufficient.

The kettle switched itself off, and she looked at
it dully while her heart wept. She had done
nothing to deserve this sort of treatment from her
aunt. Those things which she had done and of
which Ermine had so disapproved had been forced
on her by circumstances beyond her control. She
couldn't have acted in any other way. She hadn't
left willingly, and after all, what had she done that
was so reprehensible? There had been nothing
irregular or seedy about it—she had gone to live
with her husband, there was nothing wrong or
improper about that. And then she remembered,
Ermine had stolen her letters before she had gone

back to Greg. That made it all much worse.

Never at any time had she interfered with her aunt's life, and Ermine shouldn't have interfered with hers. Holding back those letters hadn't been a kind or even wise thing to do. Had she received them on time—she stopped contemplating that and closed her eyes wearily. She was so tired, so muddled—she put her head down on her arms on the counter.

When Alex woke from her doze, the clock registered five and there were tears on her face. She stiffened her spine, blew her nose on one tissue, wiped away the tears with another and covered the traces of weeping with a dab of powder from the compact in her bag. Then she reached for a mug, spooned instant coffee into it and switched the kettle back on. She was sitting at the counter sipping her coffee when she heard Ermine's key in the lock and then the light tap of feet as her aunt came straight down the passage to the bedroom and after a moment or so, came back to the kitchen door.

'Alex, dear, how lovely to see you!' and Alex looked up in surprise. There was absolutely nothing in her aunt's face or voice but pleasure. It was almost impossible to believe that she had stolen important letters.

'I let myself in—I still have a key. I know I should have given it to you, but you don't mind?' She heard herself saying it in her usual calm voice, and that surprised her as well.

'Mind? Of course I don't mind.' Ermine came across to the counter. 'What's that you're drinking, that awful instant coffee stuff? Oh, you shouldn't. You should have made the proper thing or better still, a pot of tea. I'll make one now for both of us. Go and sit in a sensible chair, dear—I can't think why you bought these stools, they're quite useless.'

Alex went to sit at the table and when her aunt came across with the tea, she took the two envelopes out of her bag and laid them down on the melamine top. 'Why?' she asked quietly.

Ermine glanced at the envelopes and then back at her niece, her face a picture of innocence. 'Why what, dear?'

'Why did you hide these letters from me?'

'These letters—may I?' Her aunt took them up, deliberately read both and then handed them back with a slight smile. 'I didn't, dear—I've never seen them before.'

For a second Alex almost believed her, but then she recalled Lucy's indignant blue eyes. It had to be either Ermine or Lucy, and she was sure it hadn't been her sister.

'Yes, you did, Ermine—Lucy found them when she helped you move your things down. Last night, this morning even, I'd have given you the benefit of the doubt, but not now. I met Lucy for lunch . . .'

'Lucy!' Ermine was triumphant. 'There's your culprit!' Her eyes glittered green and there were high spots of colour in her cheeks which, like Alex's, were normally pale. 'Lucy always was a wicked girl, irresponsible, undisciplined and quite ungovernable. It's just the sort of thing she'd do.'

'No, not Lucy,' Alex shook her head. 'You can't

put the blame for this on her, it's *not* the sort of thing she'd do.'

Ermine poured tea with a perfectly steady hand and her face twisted in a mask of pity. 'I don't suggest for one moment that Lucy would deliberately take your letters, you're jumping to conclusions, and I blame your sister, she's poisoned your mind. You say those letters went astray—possibly she picked them up, intending to give them to you, and then she forgot all about it. You know how scatterbrained she is. Then, when it was too late, she hid them to save getting into trouble. Don't let your imagination run away with you.'

'Nothing's running away with me,' Alex said quietly as she took the proffered cup of tea. It was quite extraordinary that she and her aunt could sit so calmly, one on either side of the table, drinking tea as if there was nothing wrong. 'Lucy said she found these among your things and I believe her, she's always been painfully honest even when it hurt, and she had no reason to lie. It wasn't Lucy who disliked Greg, who disapproved of me marrying him.' She raised her head and looked straight at her aunt. 'I want to know why you did it. I want to know what I've done to you which would entitle you to do this to me.'

Ermine was obstinate in her denial. 'I didn't—it was Lucy. It's just the sort of thing . . .'

'No!' Alex returned vehemently. 'It's not the sort of thing Lucy'd do and you know it. If she had picked them up and forgotten them, she would have brought them to me even if it had been a year later. She's only ever lied to me once, she'd never do it again. Now tell me why.'

Ermine's fingers tightened on the handle of her cup and she abandoned pretence. 'I did it for the best!' she almost spat the words across the table. 'You were just getting over it, settling down, and I didn't want that unsuitable marriage of yours starting up again. He treated you abominably, you know he did. I warned you against him when I first met him, but you wouldn't listen to me. I took that first letter because I knew that in time you'd forget him, and when the second one came, I took that as well. He'd been gone over a year and I didn't want him coming back into our lives and upsetting things just when they were getting back to normal. I wasn't going to let you make a fool of yourself all over again. Because that's what you became when you met him—a fool! You couldn't or wouldn't see the sort of man he was.'

Alex listened to Ermine's voice rising to an hysterical pitch and tried not to hear the things she was saying. She was successful in blocking out a lot, but several hurtful things came through clearly.

'I wanted it to be just you and me; after Lucy was gone, we would have been so happy. There wouldn't have been any need to let my little flat on the ground floor, we could have lived economically and had that and all this place as well. Lived properly, as we did when your parents, my brother and his wife, your mother were alive. Actually, the house should have been mine, not yours, it should never have been left to you, and Lucy and I would never have done what you did, let it out to strangers as soon as you were old enough to sign it away. Greg was bad for you, Alex—marrying him was a great mistake. He was notorious, notorious, I tell you—no one woman would ever satisfy him. He's a libertine—I told him to his face that he'd marry you over my dead body and he laughed at me, laughed! *Him* with his women, a different one in bed with him every night of the week. How you could stomach him, I don't know—he's indecent!'

'I love him!' Alex had to shout to make herself heard.

'Love!' Ermine snorted disdainfully. 'You can't call what you had love. It's disgusting. I thought, when you realised what sort of a man he was, that no woman was safe from him, I thought you'd be sensible, stay here with me . . .'

The tirade went on and on. Every little petty grievance, every imagined humiliation over the years spilled from her aunt's lips in a steady corrosive stream, but Alex hardly heard them. Her mind had closed down and she was fully occupied in keeping her temper in the face of extreme provocation. When her aunt started to attack Lucy, she tried to interrupt, to stop the infernal catechism of faults, but Ermine paid no attention to the interruption, continuing as though she hadn't spoken.

At last Alex stood up and started collecting her bag and gloves, eyeing her aunt with a mixture of disbelief and sorrow.

'I'm going now.' She raised her voice and the tone of it, rather sharp and disdainful, seemed to pierce Ermine's recital of her catalogue of hurts. One point had become stuck in Alex's mind and she decided to settle it now. 'You want this house. You can have it—or as much of it as I can give

you. I can't give you Lucy's share, I'm not allowed
to do that, but you can have mine and welcome.'
She snapped off the words sharply. 'Sort out the
rest with Lucy—I don't think I could bear to see
you for quite a long time. But don't forget, Lucy's
getting married and Robert will have something to
say about it . . .'

'Ready to leave, Alex?' She was interrupted by
Greg's lazy tones from where he was lounging
against the frame of the kitchen door. He sounded
lazy and he looked lazy and quite composed, as if
walking into the middle of a full-scale battle
between two warring women was an everyday
occurrence to him. He was self-possessed and
seemed quite at home, the acrid atmosphere of
dispute didn't affect him at all.

Alex glared at him. He had no right to come
interfering just when she was getting the hang of
dealing with Ermine. She envied him that self-
possession and envy sharpened her voice. 'How
did you get in here?' she demanded. 'How did you
know I'd be here?'

'I'm a thoughtful man, my dear. Go and wait
for me in the car, there's a good girl. I'll only be a
few minutes.' And because she suddenly realised
she was at the end of her tether, that any further
outburst from Ermine would send her into a
screaming fury, she went.

Outside on the pavement it was cool and
refreshing, and she lifted her face to the softly
damp breeze with gratitude, feeling it flow across
her forehead like a soothing balm. The pale sun
was already low in the sky and casting shadows,
and she was shocked to realise that it was past six

o'clock. She was desperately hungry, her attempt to eat lunch had been a miserable failure and her stomach, now accustomed to substantial meals, rumbled protestingly. And she was thirsty. She would have sold her eye teeth for a cup of tea—but she was also mildly triumphant.

Nobody could accuse her of behaving like a frightened rabbit, although Ermine had given her good cause. She had tried to be calm and dignified and she congratulated herself that she'd succeeded, at least until the final moments when her temper had started to fray around the edges and she had found it necessary to clench her hands tightly to stop herself resorting to physical violence.

Alex climbed in the car and sat very still. She wanted to cry, cry for the quiet, understanding, loving aunt who had disappeared in a rage of vindictive jealousy this afternoon and who would now never return. Self-pity, she scolded herself. If she cried, it wouldn't be for anything Ermine had said, it would be because she had seen at last the real woman who lived behind the quiet mask. The woman who could rail and rant about fancied wrongs, who could stoop to stealing letters and feel justified in doing so and who was so full of bitterness—and stupid with it!

Whether she wanted or not, the tears poured down Alex's cheeks and she licked at their saltiness when they reached her mouth, so that she didn't notice Greg until he got into the car and pulled swiftly away from the kerb.

'Stop that!' he called peremptorily, and handed her a large handkerchief. 'Mop yourself up, you look a sight.'

She mopped, and when she had collected herself a little, 'There's no need for you to be offensive! I've just had a shattering experience.'

'And you want me to feel sorry for you.' His face, staring through the windscreen, was a mask of non-expression. 'I don't, and you'll oblige me by not talking any more. There's a lot of traffic and I want to get home as soon as possible, I can't concentrate on the road and your self-inflicted sorrows, not both at the same time.'

Bidden to be silent, Alex complied. She huddled down in her seat, pulling the opulent collar of the mink more closely to cover her ears, and closed her eyes. One couldn't live in a welter of misery for ever, she consoled herself. Some time, some day, things were bound to get better. It was just a matter of hanging on long enough, living for the future and blocking out the worst parts of the past—or better still, blocking out all the past, since the nice parts invariably led to memories that weren't so good. Like rubbish, the whole lot should be burned!

Her tears started again, but she choked them back and sat dry-eyed. After this was all over, after Greg had finished with her, she would make a fresh start. It would be a lonely one, Lucy would be wrapped up in her new husband and her new home, and Ermine—she would have to forget the closeness of that relationship for quite a while. She and her aunt might never get back on to the old footing, it would need a lot of understanding before they achieved even a small fraction of their previous closeness.

And Greg would have no part in that new start.

She didn't want a practical-type marriage, one that was founded on good sense. It would be too cerebral for her, like some sort of computer-type emotion.

It would be better to begin again completely afresh, to wipe out every memory, to be born twenty-six years old and with no past to look back on or to grieve over.

Her miserable musings were interrupted when Greg garaged the car and practically towed her up to and into the flat. He dumped her unceremoniously in the lounge, bade her sit quietly while he made some coffee and went off with the implied threat—'After you've had a drink and pulled yourself together, I've a few things to say to you.'

'Tea,' she protested, 'I'd rather have tea,' but he stalked out of the room without giving any sign that he'd heard her. However, when the drink came, it *was* tea, a lot of it, very sweet and milky in a huge stoneware mug. Alex sipped at it and wrinkled her nose expressively.

'Too sweet?' Greg didn't apologise and he didn't sit down, he stood over her—a tall, dark, menacing figure. Alex cringed inwardly. He was in a temper and she didn't think she could cope, she was too tired. He waited until she set the mug down.

'I believe you've just received some letters I sent you.' He held out a hand. 'Give!'

'Why?'

'I collect foreign stamps—remind me to show you my album some time.' From the tone of his voice, she knew he didn't intend to discuss the letters with her, and her fingers tightened on her handbag. 'Come on,' he ordered tersely, 'hand them over—and don't try to tell me you haven't got them, you're hanging on to that bag as though it contained the Crown Jewels.'

'They're my letters.' Alex was a trifle mutinous, but she handed them over, and as she did so, he caught at her hand and examined it.

'I see you're without a wedding ring again.' His thumb stroked her ringless finger with a caressing movement. 'You're a very expensive lady when it comes to wedding rings, you either throw them away or grow out of them. Perhaps it would be cheaper if I bought them by the dozen or put in a standing order for one a month.' Alex suspected he was trying to change the subject, get away from the letters, and she was quite willing for the subject to be changed.

'I never wanted or asked you to spend your money on me,' she snapped, 'but this time, you can put the flag up, because I've got it right!' She fumbled once more in her bag and brought out the little box. 'Here are the pieces,' she said triumphantly. 'I expect you'll be able to sell them back to the jeweller.'

'Hmm!' He tossed the box down on to the table. 'I suppose I should be glad you didn't throw that into the river as well—now be a good girl and go and get us something to eat. Your idea of a ham sandwich for lunch saved a lot of time, but it's left me hungry. And perhaps it might help if you found the correct book and re-read the marriage service. There's a bit in it about "forsaking all other". Think about that while you're cooking something, it'll take your mind off trivialities.'

Alex slipped past him through the door and thought of an answer to that one. 'That phrase applies to both parties, I believe,' she said haughtily and with her nose in the air. 'Or if it doesn't—it should!' And she made what she hoped was a victorious exit.

Once in the kitchen and with the door firmly closed against her husband, her mood of victory deserted her. Greg wasn't so much a tower of strength as a block of granite. He couldn't understand or sympathise with weakness and he expected everybody to be as impervious to hurt—as strong-minded, practical and sure of themselves as he was.

But this time, he could damn well break his 'no explanations' rule. There were things she wanted to know, like—how had he known she was with Ermine? How had he known about the letters? Alex wanted some answers to those questions, she wanted to know why he had asked for a divorce, or offered her one, she wanted to know a lot of things, and she wasn't going to take a supercilious rise of an eyebrow or a refusal to discuss lying down.

CHAPTER TEN

ALEX banged around the kitchen, swearing at the inoffensive gadgets in a manner quite unlike her usual calm, quiet way of working. Irritability, brought on by hunger, an over-exposure to family scenes and the shock of the letters coupled with overtiredness made her fingers less than deft. In any case, it was the wrong time for a meal. She slapped an eggbox on to the counter with an angry grunt—it was an hour too early for dinner and her larder, while not exactly bare, wasn't in its usual healthy state. She gloomed over the time she had wasted waiting in the basement flat for Ermine to come home. In that time, she could have done quite a lot of shopping, bought fresh food, and then she would have had something to cook with instead of having to resort to frozen stuff and tins.

She speculated on various quick and filling dishes and had to abandon her favourite, a Spanish omelette. For that she needed left-overs, and since their dinner last evening had been an equally makeshift affair, there were no left-overs to make the omelette filling. She would have to resort to the freezer once more.

She pawed through the contents of the deep freeze and emerged with her fingers frozen to the bone and a tray of pork chops. She could put them in the micro-wave oven while they were still rigid with frost, and when they were cooked through

they could go under the grill to brown off.
Hunger got the better of her and she began to take
an interest in what she was doing. With grim
determination, she retrieved the despised sliced
ham from the fridge, sandwiched a particularly
thick slice between two pieces of bread, anointed
the whole thing with mustard and chewed at it to
still her hunger pangs.

Damn everybody! she muttered under her
breath. Damn Ermine for causing so much
trouble, for giving her a sleepless night, for getting
her so wound up that she hadn't been able to sleep
or eat properly and had forgotten about the
shopping. Damn Lucy for finding those letters and
for sending them to her—without them she, Alex,
would have been able to go on with this marriage,
thinking it was all roses and rainbows for ever—
and last of all, damn Greg for wanting food when
she felt so disinclined to prepare it. Longingly, she
thought of a deserted, desert island as she slid a
frozen blackcurrant tart into the conventional
oven.

The telephone rang in the hall just as she was
reaching her plastic apron from its hook, and she
opened the door a fraction and listened un-
ashamedly. She didn't learn a thing from the one-
sided conversation except that Greg's impatience
and lack of tolerance was restricted to herself. He
sounded quite goodhumoured to whoever was on
the other end of the line.

'Yes, of course . . . No, no bother at all . . . No,
not tonight . . . I don't know about tomorrow.'
Alex heard him laugh and then—'No, don't ring
here, I'll ring you,' and he hung up.

Alex banged the door shut in sheer frustration and went back to the counter, where she made a big thing of restoring the eggbox to the fridge, taking out a carton of cream instead to whip up for a tart topping. When Greg came into the kitchen, she was standing with the cream already in a bowl and her finger on the start button of the electric blender.

'Lucy,' he announced. 'I told her not to bother coming round here tonight.'

'Good!' Alex screwed up the empty cream carton and rammed it viciously into the waste disposal unit which she held open with her foot. 'I don't feel sociable,' then she rammed her finger home on the button of the blender, an act which totally destroyed any further chance of communication.

When her husband had gone back to the lounge, she finished her preparations, the chops were put under the grill with halved tomatoes and the blackcurrant tart was prayed for—that it would be heated all the way through and not come to the table with a lump of ice at its centre. It wouldn't be an exciting meal, but it should taste all right, and she stirred cream and wine into stock to thicken it while she tried to recall what exactly had been said in the marriage service.

Had she really vowed to forsake all other? It seemed rather a sweeping vow, but she could remember very little of what had happened that day and she was almost totally in the dark about what she'd promised. She recalled balking at 'obey' which she had said would reduce her to serfdom, but in any case, it wasn't necessary for her to remember. Greg had said 'look in the book', but that wasn't necessary either. She knew she could rely on his memory, his damned photographic, infallible memory. If he said she had, then she had!

They ate the meal in near silence, and when they had finished, Greg carried the coffee tray into the lounge, coming back to rescue her from her self-imposed isolation in the kitchen. She was clearing away and stacking used crockery and cutlery in the dishwasher while wondering what else she could find to occupy her until bedtime.

'Come along,' he brooked no opposition and his fingers closed round her arm, compelling her. 'We've a bit of talking to do.'

'I don't feel like talking,' Alex muttered. 'I've had enough of that today to last me the rest of the week.'

'Then you can sit quietly and listen to me.' He was sweetly reasonable as he steered her to the couch, gave her a little push which upset her balance and watched as she subsided on to the fat squabs. 'For instance,' he poured coffee and handed her a cup, 'what do you want to do about a wedding ring, would you like another new one or would you prefer to have the last one repaired and made bigger? They can do that, you know, and you won't even notice the joins. It's your ring, so you can decide.'

'Neither.' She closed her eyes, sounding weary and uninterested. 'I don't want anything from you at all . . .'

'You don't want anything?' Her head was turned away from him so that she couldn't see him, but she could hear the amusement in his voice and it stirred her into life.

'What I want is impossible.' She turned her head to glare at him. 'I'd like to be able to go back in time, back to before I met you. I'd like to start all over again . . .'

'And you'd make the same mistakes all over again,' Greg snorted derisively.

'No, I shouldn't,' she raised her chin defiantly. 'I wouldn't marry you, that's for starters. Everything was plain sailing until I did that. It was my biggest mistake . . .'

'Then why didn't you do something about it?' he demanded. 'You can forget that infantile drivel about wanting to start all over again, you sound like science fiction in search of a time machine!'

'If I'd had that letter, either of those letters, when I should have had them, I *would* have done something about it,' she flared. 'And that's something I want—I want to know how you knew about them, how you knew where I'd be this afternoon. You can sniff all you want, but I want an explanation.'

'Lucy,' he ignored her bad temper. 'Thank heaven for one sensible member of your family! She was worried about you, so she did the right thing, she phoned me and told me about it, which is what you should have done when you received them.'

'Lucy? But she said she wouldn't tell . . .'

'She said she wouldn't tell Robert, she didn't say she wouldn't tell me,' he pointed out.

'I suppose you thought I'd received them?' Alex hazarded.

'Yes, and I wondered what in hell you were playing at—Oh, I forgot, you don't know the whole story yet, let me enlighten you. A week or so before I wrote you that second letter, I received one from your sweet little aunt. I have it here,' he tapped his pocket, 'but I shan't show it to you, not unless you insist. Will you take my word for it if I tell you what it contained?'

'Of course.' She looked at him blankly. 'It's your one good point, you don't lie about anything.'

'Thank you so much!' he retorted sardonically. 'I'm glad you've found one good thing about me. Your aunt's letter was short and sweet—you'd got over me, you'd discovered what a terrible mistake you'd made, you'd met a man, one you could really love—a worthy man—you wanted to marry him—need I go on?'

'But I didn't—I hadn't!' she protested, and then, 'but *you* did, you wrote that horrid letter and you sent evidence . . .'

'I thought it was what you wanted, and my girl-friend at that time was quite willing to help, and your aunt was imploring me, on your behalf. She said you were too proud, too sensitive to ask yourself, so I complied. How was I to know you were in ignorance of the whole affair? And as for going there today, did you think you could deal with a thing like this? Your aunt is well named, Ermine Winter, but just remember, it's only Ermine in winter, at other times of the year the animal's called a stoat. You were out of your class when you tangled with her, my dear,' his tone was scathing. 'Little Goody Two Shoes, off on her own private crusade. Thank God for Lucy!'

Alex sat silent, almost in shock, while she assimilated the information. She didn't want to believe it, not any of it, certainly not the part about Ermine's letter, but she knew it was true, that if she demanded to see it it would be exactly as he said. He'd read it, and in one year or ten years' time he would be able to reproduce it word for word. Greg abandoned his stance over her and dropped down beside her on the couch, taking her by the shoulders and giving her a good shake so that she came out of the nightmare to look at him with dazed eyes.

'So you see, I was right, you sat back for three years and did nothing. Why was that?' He gave her another shake. 'I'll tell you why, Mrs Mallus, it was because you didn't want to alter anything. Underneath all those layers of self-deception, you liked being married to me. You liked it when we were first married, and although you have this crazy idea that I'm some sort of male stud, you're still liking it now. That's why you've done nothing about it, and if you'll stop wriggling like an eel, I'll prove it to you.'

'No!' She pushed away from him, stiffening her back, pressing her hands against his chest and using every scrap of strength she possessed to keep him at what she hoped was a safe distance. In another few moments, if he kept up his attack, she would, she knew, collapse against him, be as weak and willing as any other stupid fool in love. She tried to whip herself into a tempest of self-disgust at her own weakness.

There was nothing different about her, she

screamed a silent accusation at herself—she was exactly the same soft, spineless material as all the rest of his conquests except in so far as she was willing to do it for free—whereas, with the others, she supposed, she hoped he was expected to demonstrate his appreciation in a fairly concrete form.

As for his suggestion that she deceived herself, that didn't come into it at all. Her love for him was one thing about which she'd never pretended, all she had ever done was to try to hide it from him. She wasn't ashamed of it, she had only concealed it from him so that he shouldn't use it against her.

'Oh yes,' Greg contradicted her, while one of his hands was busy at the neckline of the soft green woollen dress she was wearing. His fingers flicked buttons from their buttonholes and then pushed the stuff from her shoulders. 'It seems to me, my dear, that there's only one way to settle this, and I'm taking it with or without your permission. I want you, you want me, so what's there to fight about?'

His hand found her breast and at his touch she collapsed, tears welling into her eyes. 'It's not a weeping matter, sweetheart,' he murmured in her ear, and then his mouth was on hers and she was lost. Her hands which had been striving to push him away now slid up around his shoulders and as her lips parted beneath his, she tightened her fingers in his hair, feeling the wiriness of it, clutching convulsively, holding his head down to hers so that the sweetness should last for as long as possible.

'Mmm.' Greg sounded pleased and appreciative when he at last raised his mouth from hers. 'But no, my love,' and he smiled down at her flushed face and into her dreamy eyes. 'It's barely nine o'clock, too early to go to bed, and I'm past the age when making love uncomfortably on a couch was attractive. We'll control our animal passions until a more seemly time, shall we? There's quite a lot to talk about, several points we have to iron out first,' and as she moved to be free of him, to remove his marauding hand which was cupping and teasing at her breast—'Don't move away! If you keep quite still where you are, you'll find it very comfortable. It's what's known as building up to a crescendo.'

Alex sighed with regret. To Greg, she must be as transparent as water, she always had been, perhaps. She wished she was stronger, more able to hide her feelings, but wishing for the impossible was useless. This, apparently, was the moment of truth. There was little left for her but complete honesty and something inside of her was insisting that she be truthful. At least if she was he couldn't accuse her of self-deception. 'I love you,' she said with a sad little dignity. 'Please understand, Greg. I don't want to, it puts me at such a disadvantage, but I do.'

'I know, darling.' He pulled her even closer and she buried her hot face in the front of his shirt. 'Did you think I didn't?' Beneath her cheek, she felt a soft rumble of laughter. 'You wouldn't give yourself, not to me or any other man, without that. It would never be enough for you, the pleasure, the satisfaction . . .'

'You accused me of treating you like a one-night stand,' she reminded him, and felt his arms tighten and his body grow taut against hers.

'I was angry with you, Alex, and not only with you, with myself and the whole damn set-up. You're not stingy with your loving, it's one of your most attractive features. You don't just take, you give, and you'd just given me a night of generosity, and then the phone rang and it all collapsed around me. Even the memory of it was spoiled. Your aunt wanted you, and immediately you forgot about me. That's what I meant about forsaking all other. Suddenly I didn't matter to you any more, and I won't have that. I have to come first, if you've any love left over after that, you can spread it on your family. Why don't you want to love me?'

'You know why.' Alex opened her eyes wide. 'You *do*!'

'Yes,' he made no attempt to evade the accusation. 'As you say, I know why—but we'll leave that point for a while, if you please. It's rather a sticky point and you've been stuck on it for far too long. You'd do better to concentrate on the broad outlines, work on the future. The past is gone and it never was all that important anyway.'

'But it is!' she wailed, sitting upright in his restraining arm and making a valiant attempt to smooth out her rumpled, disorderly appearance. 'It's a very important part.'

'Not a bit of it,' he frowned at her. 'It's a minor detail. Let's get down to basics. Item one—you love me, which is very encouraging when we take it one step further. You've at last admitted it, although it had to be wrung out of you. So now we have a basis of some hope for the future. Item two,' he placed a long finger under her chin, tilting her head and forcing her to look at him, 'are you going to stay with me of your own sweet will?'

'I don't have much option.' Alex wriggled her chin free and looked down at her hands, becoming excessively interested in a small speck which she discovered on one of her nails. 'I'm not like you, I can't compartmentalise emotions. Oh, it's no use talking to you about it, you go in for logic and clear thinking, and I can't think clearly about what I feel. I love you and I'm your wife, so I expect I'll stay with you, but whether I'll be happy doing it, I don't know. It might hurt too much.'

Greg raised his eyebrows. 'At least I know what I want and I know how to go about getting it,' he pointed out. 'I'm not like you, bogged down in a layer of self-protection. Let's move on to item three, which is your family, and in particular, your aunt. I've reservations about her, she's a very determined lady and you're no match for her. She'll be trotting round, dropping little bits of poison in your ears, she's far too clever and devious for you, I think you'd better not see her any more. I shall forbid it!'

He sounded so insufferably superior that Alex reacted violently. She had no intention of going to see her aunt—well, not for a long time—but as soon as she heard Greg laying down the law, she became bellicose.

'You forbid? How dare you! You're nothing but a dictator!' And then she became sickeningly superior herself. 'You may be a whale at history,

but you know nothing about psychology. Those
letters of yours, both of them, they were insults,
and the second was worse than the first—at least
that's the way I see it. How would you have liked
it if I'd sent something like that to you? Times,
places and names sent to a solicitor and the
implication that if you couldn't stomach *my*
infidelity, you could use the information to get a
divorce. It's a pity I didn't get that letter, I'd have
divorced you at once! And as for not seeing
Ermine again, I shall see her whenever I please—
I'll have to anyway, I'm giving her my share of the
house.'

'Over my dead body!' Greg dragged her round
to face him and she saw his face set in a scowl.
'There's a lot of *our* money invested in that house,
and *we* aren't going to take a loss because your
aunt wants her name on the list for jury service as
a householder. At least then we'll have something
for our old age, and by the way you go through
finger jewellery, we'll need it. Which only leaves us
with item four, which I consider the least
important, although you will keep harping on it.'

He pulled her closer and bent his head to brush
his mouth across her cheek. 'Look, it's nearly ten
o'clock—we could go to bed now with perfect
propriety.'

'Go to bed?' Alex wrinkled her nose. 'But I'm
entitled . . .' She watched his face darken. 'Damn
you, Greg,' she almost snarled. 'Why can't you
lower your standards a little? Why must I always
have to take you on trust? Don't you realise
how . . .' She looked up at him, knowing he didn't
understand, that he probably never would. 'You

don't feel a bit guilty, do you, not ever. I'm not as insensitive as you are. An explanation . . .' she tried to make it a firm demand, but it came out hesitantly.

'The hell I will!' Greg released her and pushed her to the other end of the couch. 'Why should I make it easy for you, you pigheaded little moron? Just so you can go to bed with me and wake up tomorrow morning with a clear conscience instead of feeling defiled!'

'How dare you!' Alex was angrily indignant. 'I'm not a moron, that's an insult to my intelligence!'

'What intelligence?' he sneered. 'Intelligence implies thought, and that's one thing you never did, think! If you had, you might have asked yourself a few questions instead of storming at me as you've been doing. When I wrote that second letter, I was at the end of my tether. I'd waited and waited, but you didn't come, you didn't write, you did nothing! You went on with your life as though I'd never existed or as if I was a pair of shoes or a hat you'd bought, disliked and pushed in the back of a cupboard. Damn you, woman, you were my wife, and you showed as much feeling as a bloody statue! You want explanations—well, you can have them. I had myself photographed with any woman I could find, I encouraged every scandal-mongering gossip writer to splash me in any paper which would print the muck, and you didn't even blink!'

'And it was all innocent?' Alex pushed herself back against the cushions.

'No, it damn well wasn't, but what there was

was a commercial arrangement. To be crude, I paid for it. I'm human, not like you, half an iceberg, and I was at the stage where I didn't care any more. Either you were in my life, were my life, or you were out of it. I received your aunt's letter and I answered it and sat back to wait again, waiting for divorce papers to be served on me, but that didn't happen either, so,' he moved in on her, catching at her shoulders, 'I decided to come back. If you weren't going to divorce me, then you could get back to being my wife. You say you love me, but what sort of love is it that won't bend a little bit, refuses to even try to understand?'

'And would you have taken me back if I'd . . .'

'It would have been hard,' he admitted, 'but yes, I'd have had no option either. I love you, my dear, it's not living without you.'

'That's the first time you've ever said that, I think,' she marvelled as she softened against him. 'It makes the world of difference. But,' and she sighed although happiness was making her lightheaded, 'there were so many others, I'd had so many predecessors.'

'Not so many,' he grinned. 'These things always get exaggerated, and I never married any of them. You said that I didn't say I loved you, but why on earth did you think I married you? Because you were a good typist?'

'Could have been,' and she grinned back at him cheekily. 'What time is it?'

'Bedtime,' he said definitely, 'and before I forget, I think I've found us a house. Do you want to talk about that?'

'Not tonight,' she said dreamily. Life was

looking very promising, as if the roses and rainbows were here to stay. 'I think we've talked enough for one day.'

'Two minds with but a single thought.' Greg pulled her to her feet, his hand lingering about her waist. 'We at last agree about something. Is it enough to base a happy marriage on?'

'Oh, I think so,' and then very softly, 'Do I have to say "Please"?'

'Yes, of course,' his arm tightened until she could hardly breathe, 'and "Thank you"!'

Alex woke to the thin light of dawn and remembered the questions. They had come to her in the darkness, but she had put them aside. She had been warm and comfortable, Greg's arm was close about her and his chest was making a very satisfactory pillow. But now those two questions were back with her, pricking at her mind, and she needed the answers.

She raised herself on her elbow and looked down at her husband's sleeping face. 'Are you awake?' she asked.

'No.' Greg didn't open his eyes as he answered her. 'What's the matter? I hope you don't want to start talking again.'

'Yes,' she ignored his sleepy grumble. 'I thought of a couple of things during the night . . .'

'You were *thinking* during the night?' He sounded as though it was unbelievable. 'Not enough work to do—Night's for—er—sleeping . . .'

'But it's important,' she pulled his hair. 'Are you listening to me?'

'Do I have a choice?' He opened his eyes at last. 'What time is it? Five o'clock!' he groaned. 'Alex, I refuse to start talking at dawn.'

'Why did Ermine hide that second letter?' she interrupted swiftly before he could close his eyes again. 'Greg, please listen to me. She must have known it was about a divorce . . .'

'Mmm,' he grumbled sleepily. 'But she had to hide it, it might have mentioned her letter to me—she wouldn't have wanted you to know about that. May I go back to sleep now, please?'

'No, you can't, I haven't finished yet.' Once more she grabbed a handful of hair and pulled. 'The ring—you said it was engraved, what was it?'

'See for yourself, lazybones,' he yawned.

'Was it just the date and initials?'

'Go and look.' He attempted to turn over, but she wouldn't let him, 'Look for yourself,' he protested. 'You've no excuse this time, you have your specs and the box of bits is where we left it on the table last night.'

'But I don't want to get up yet.' Alex snuggled down close to him. 'Why should I? You can tell me.'

'No, knowledge should be searched for, not handed to you on a plate.' He closed his eyes firmly, and with a sigh she struggled up and reached for a robe, shrugging it around her shoulders. Regretfully, she slid out of bed to patter on bare feet to the lounge. When she returned her eyes were full of a soft laughter.

'Greg, you're a romantic,' she accused. 'Only a romantic would have "FOR EVER" inscribed on a wedding ring!'

'Hmm, wishful thinking—the record's not been too good so far. The first one only lasted three weeks and the second one not much longer.'

Alex dropped the robe on the floor and slid back into the warmth of his arms, which tightened round her in a reassuring way. 'I think, if you don't mind, I'll have another new ring. It'll be the third, and third time lucky.'

'Luck has nothing to do with it, it's hard work and understanding that makes a . . .' but she kissed him into silence.

'Nice work,' he murmured when she raised her head. 'Keep it up, my girl, and we'll make a success of it yet.'

'Are you going back to sleep?' she enquired softly, and his hand slid from her waist down to rest on the silken softness of her hip, tightening and drawing her towards him.

'No!'

A PASSIONATE SHEPHERD TO HIS LOVE

Greg, the hero of Jeneth Murrey's Romance, seems to be fond of using deliberate misquotes to tease Alexandra. On one occasion Greg says to Alex, "Come sleep with me and be my love," a misquote from a famous poem by sixteenth-century English dramatist Christopher Marlowe. In case you're not familiar with the correct quote, here it is, along with Marlowe's lovely poem entitled "A Passionate Shepherd to His Love," from which it is taken.

Come live with me and be my love,
And we will all the pleasures prove
That valleys, groves, hills and fields,
Woods, or steepy mountain yields.

And we will sit upon the rocks,
Seeing the shepherds feed their flocks,
By shallow rivers to whose falls
Melodious birds sing madrigals.

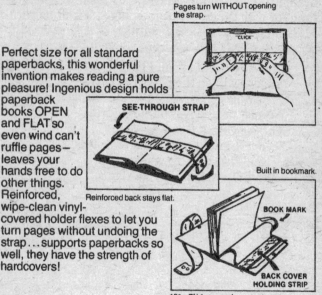